T0266052

The Burroughs File

William S. Burroughs
THE BURROUGHS FILE

CITY LIGHTS BOOKS
San Francisco

10 9

Cover photograph: Burroughs coming across yage plants in jungle near Macao, Colombia, 1953. Photographer unknown.

Design: Nancy J. Peters, Kim McCloud
Editing & Typography: V. Vale, Re/Search

Library of Congress Cataloging-in-Publication Data

Burroughs, William S., 1914-1997
    The Burroughs File.

    I. Title.
  PS3552.U75B8   1984   813'.54 84-4216
  ISBN: 0-87286-158-9 (cloth)
  ISBN: 0-87286-152-X (pbk)

CITY LIGHTS BOOKS are edited by Lawrence Ferlinghetti and Nancy J. Peters and published at the City Lights Bookstore, 261 Columbus Avenue, San Francisco, CA 94133.

CONTENTS

Introductory Notes *by James Grauerholz* 9
Burroughs in Tangier *by Paul Bowles* 15
Whoever Can Pick up a Frying Pan Owns Death *by Alan Ansen* 17

THE WHITE SUBWAY 27

Photograph from Book of Hours

Unfinished Cigarette 29
Distant Hand Lifted 34
The Conspiracy 39
Ancient Face Gone Out 44
Who is the Third That Walks Beside You? 50
The Last Post *Danger Ahead* 53
Palm Sunday Tape 56
The Beginning is Also the End 62
The Coldspring News 67
Who Is the Walks Beside You Written 3rd? 72
St. Louis Return 79
Composite Text 90

THE OLD MOVIES 95

Photograph from Book of Hours

Word Authority More Habit Forming than Heroin 97
So Who Owns Death TV 99
Abstract 106
Fear and the Monkey 110
Distant Heels 112
Pages from Chaos 115
23 Skiddoo 118
Old Photographer 122
The Inferential Kid 128
Last Awning Flaps on the Pier 134
The Bay of Pigs 136
File Ticker Tape 145
The Moving Times 150

PAGES FROM SCRAPBOOKS 153

Photograph from (with John Brady) John Brady's Book

Publishers' Note 155
The Old Farmer's Almanac 156
Book of Hours 158
John Brady's Book 180

THE RETREAT DIARIES 185

Photograph from Book of Hours

COBBLE STONE GARDENS 209

Photograph (with his father and brother Mort)

James Grauerholz

SOME INTRODUCTORY NOTES

Around 1958, William Burroughs moved from Tangier to live in Paris, at the now-famous Beat Hotel at 9 rue Git-le-Coeur. He brought with him a trunk full of papers, from which not only *Naked Lunch* but also *The Ticket That Exploded, The Soft Machine,* and *Nova Express* were assembled over the next few years. The publication of *Naked Lunch* by Maurice Girodias' Olympia Press in Paris in 1959, coming three years after Allen Ginsberg's *Howl* (City Lights) and two years after Jack Kerouac's *On The Road* (Viking), brought Burroughs to the attention of the international literary underground.

Before this time, Burroughs' fame extended only to his circle of friends. His first book, *Junky* (Ace Books, 1953), had been written under the pseudonym of "William Lee," and was not seen at the time by very many writers and critics. But *Naked Lunch* focused worldwide attention on its author. The novel was tried for obscenity in Boston, and acquitted. It galvanized the Edinburgh Literary Conference of 1962, dividing response sharply between Mary McCarthy, Norman Mailer, Alex Trocchi and others, who praised the book as an American masterpiece, and the many other critics who assailed it as "the merest trash, not worth a second glance," etc. To this day, Burroughs' work continues to provoke violent critical controversy, but his recent election to the American Academy and Institute of Arts and Letters provides some measure of his growing acceptance by the "literary establishment."

During the early 1960s, Burroughs was developing the "cut-up" theory of writing in collaboration with his friend, the artist Brion Gysin. The "cut-up" is essentially the application of the montage technique, as found in painting, to the process of writing. Aleatory techniques of literary composition were nothing new; Lewis Carroll had hinted at the idea, and Tristan Tzara's poem pulled in pieces from a hat is now famous. But in the hands of Burroughs and Gysin, and applied to the images of popular culture and the midden-heap of modern literature, the "cut-up" was a powerful artistic tool.

At this same time, as we all know now, a worldwide cultural revolution began to stir. After *Naked Lunch,* Burroughs began to receive numerous requests for material from the "little mags" that sprang up during the period. In fact, the *William S. Burroughs Bibliography, 1953-1973* (University of Virginia Press) reads like a *Who's Who* of little magazines and underground publishers around the world. Burroughs' principal literary output between 1962 and 1969 appeared in these obscure places, and most of the pieces collected in *The Burroughs File* date from that period. *The Wild Boys* (Grove Press, 1970) marked his return to full-length works.

Burroughs also worked with montage in his series of Scrapbooks, which he continues to create. The sample Scrapbook pages reproduced here are from the same period as the published pieces, and are used with the kind permission of Stanley and Elyse Grinstein. One can see how the collaboration with Brion Gysin, and the physical manipulation of the text, influence this period in Burroughs' writing.

We may imagine the author in the early 1960s, sitting long hours at his typewriter in his room at the Beat Hotel, or his rooms in London, answering letters from poets and little-magazine publishers all over America and Europe, sending out these bulletins of image and revolution to a world he hoped to show the writing on the wall: *Minutes To Go.* Twenty years later, the urgency remains.

1984

THE BURROUGHS FILE: Publishing History

The White Subway, Aloes seolA, 1973 (London)
   Unfinished Cigarette: *Birmingham Bulletin* 2, Autumn 1963 (Birmingham, England)
   Distant Hand Lifted: *Transatlantic Review* 15, Spring 1964 (London); *Cleft* 1, no. 2, May 1964 (Edinburgh)
   The Conspiracy: *Kulchur* 1, 1960 (New York); in *Apomorphine,* Editions l'Herne, 1969 (Paris)
   The Danish Operation: *Arcade* 1, 1964 (London); in *Cut Up,* Melzer Verlag, 1969 (Darmstadt)
   The Cut: *Arcade* 1, 1964; in *Cut Up,* 1969
   Ancient Face Gone Out: *Gnaoua* 1, Spring 1964 (Tangier)
   Who is the Third That Walks Beside You?: *Art and Literature* 2, Summer 1964 (New York); *East Village Other,* 1971 (New York); *Renaissance* 8, 1971 (San Francisco); *Organ,* July 1971 (Berkeley, Ca.); *Poudrie de Dent,* June 1973 (Paris); in *Sterminatore!,* Sugar Editore, 1969 (Milan)
   The Last Post Danger Ahead: *Lines* 6, November 1965 (New York)
   Palm Sunday Tape: *Bulletin from Nothing* 2, 1965 (San Francisco); in *Burroughs, Pelieu, Kaufman,* Editions l'Herne, 1967 (Paris); in *Sterminatore!* (op cit)
   The Beginning is Also the End: *Transatlantic Review* 14, Autumn 1963 (London)
   The Coldspring News: *The Spero* 1, no. 1, Fenian Head Centre Press, 1965 (Flint, Michigan); *Krea* 6, S'Hertogenbosch, 1965 (Amsterdam); *San Francisco Earthquake* 1, no. 4, 1968 (San Francisco); *Intrepid* 14/15, 1969 (Buffalo, N.Y.); in *Apomorphine,* l'Herne, 1969 (Paris)
   Who Is the Walks beside You Written 3rd?: *Darazt,* July 1965 (London)
   St. Louis Return: in *Acid—Neue Amerikanische Szene,* Maro Verlag, 1969 (Darmstadt); *Paris Review* 35, Fall 1965 (Paris)
   Composite Text: *Bulletin from Nothing* 1, 1965 (San Francisco); in *Sterminatore!* (op cit)
   Anyone Who Can Pick up a Frying Pan Owns Death (by Alan Ansen): *Big Table* 2, 1959 (Chicago); Parkinson, Thomas, ed., *Casebook on the Beats,* T.Y. Crowell, 1961 (New York)
   Burroughs in Tangier (by Paul Bowles): *Big Table* 2 (op cit); Parkinson, T. (op cit)

11

Die Alten Filme, edited by Carl Weissner, Maro Verlag, 1979 (Augsburg)

> Distant Heels: *Adventures in Poetry* 9, 1972 (New York); in *Mayfair Academy Series More or Less,* Urgency Press Rip-Off, 1973 (London)
>
> Pages from Chaos: *Antaeus* 2, 1971 (Tangier); cf. version in Burroughs, William S., *Cities of the Red Night,* Holt Rinehart & Winston, 19 (New York)
>
> 23 Skiddoo: *Transatlantic Review* 25, 1967 (London); cf. version in Burroughs, William S., *Exterminator/The Job*
>
> File Ticker Tape: *Insect Trust Gazette* 2, 1965 (Philadelphia); in *Burroughs, Pelieu, Kaufman* (op cit)
>
> Old Photographer (unpublished in English), The Inferential Kid (unpublished in English), The Bay of Pigs (unpublished in English)
>
> Last Awning Flaps on the Pier: *Intrepid* 5, 1965 (New York); *San Francisco Earthquake* 1, no. 2, 1968 (San Francisco); *Intrepid* 14/15, 1969 (Buffalo, N.Y.); in *Sterminatore!* (op cit)
>
> The Moving Times: *VDRSVP, Nova Broadcast* (Norman Mustill/ Jan Jacob Herman), 1969 (San Francisco, Athens, New York, Mannheim, London); *My Own Mag* (London)

The Retreat Diaries, The City Moon, City Moon Broadcast 3, 1976 (New York)

Cobble Stone Gardens, Cherry Valley Editions (edited by Charles and Pam Plymell), 1976 (New York)

THE BURROUGHS FILE

BURROUGHS IN TANGIER

By Paul Bowles

I first saw Bill Burroughs in 1953, passing along a back street of Tangier in the rain. He was on H at the time, and he didn't look very fit.

The next year he came to see me about some detail in his contract for *Junky,* in which he said he had been taken. I had paratyphoid and wasn't very helpful. It wasn't until the winter of 1955-56 that we became friends and started to see each other regularly. Naturally I had been told about him: how he practiced shooting in his room down in the Medina, and all the rest of the legend. When I got to know him I realized the legend existed in spite of him and not because of him: he didn't give a damn about it.

His life had no visible organization about it, but knowing he was an addictive type he had chosen that way of giving himself an automatic interior discipline which was far more rigorous than any he could have imposed upon himself objectively. He lived in a damp little room whose single door opened onto the garden of the Hotel Villa Muniriya. One wall of the room, his shooting gallery, was pockmarked with bullet holes. Another wall was completely covered with snapshots, most of which he had taken on a trip to the headwaters of the Amazon. I liked to hear about that voyage, and always got him to talk lengthily about it.

Going there had been part of the self-imposed discipline, since the only reason he had gone was to try the effects of a local drug called Yage, a concoction made by the Indians of the region, and which must be taken on the spot since its efficacy vanishes within a few hours after it is brewed. The point about Yage is that it is, more than any other, a group drug, its particular property being the facilitation of mental telepathy and emotional empathy among those who have taken it. He insisted that with it communication was possible with the Indians, although it made him violently ill.

15

During the two years that I saw Bill regularly in Tangier, he took only kif, majoun and alcohol. But he managed to take vast amounts of all three. The litter on his desk and under it, on the floor, was chaotic, but it consisted only of pages of *Naked Lunch,* at which he was constantly working. When he read aloud from it, at random (any sheet of paper he happened to grab would do) he laughed a good deal, as well he might, since it is very funny, but from reading he would suddenly (the paper still in hand) go into a bitter conversational attack upon whatever aspect of life had prompted the passage he had just read. The best thing about Bill Burroughs is that he always makes sense and he is always humorous, even at his most vitriolic. At any point of the night or day you might happen to catch him, you will always find that whole machine is going full blast, and that means that he is laughing or about to laugh.

He spends more money on food than most of us Tangerines, I've noticed; perhaps he has more to spend—I don't know—but the fact remains that he insists on eating well, which is part of his insistence on living just as he likes at all times. (Gertrude Stein would have called him self-indulgent; he certainly is not ever hampered by even a shadow of the feeling of guilt, ever.) He goes on his way enjoying even his own misfortunes. I've never heard him mention an experience that made him more than temporarily happy. At the Hotel Muniriya he has a Reich orgone box in which he used to sit doubled up, smoking kif. I believe he made it himself. He had a little stove in his room over which he cooked his own hashish candy, of which he was very proud, and which he distributed to anyone who was interested.

The months that Allen Ginsberg was here in Tangier, he and Bill used to sit around half the night having endless fights about literature and aesthetics. It was always Bill who attacked the intellect from all sides, which I suspect was exactly what Allen wanted to hear. Surely it was worth hearing, and worth watching too, as Bill stumbled from one side of the room to another, shouting in his cowboy voice, stirring his drink around and around without stopping, with his index and middle finger, and with two or three kif cigarettes lighted simultaneously but lying in different ashtrays which he visited on his way around the room.

1959

ANYONE WHO CAN PICK UP A FRYING PAN OWNS DEATH

by Alan Ansen

Agatha Christie, somewhere, making fun of the plot of a hypothetical modern play, says that the young hero is actually a sort of saint: he robs, he commits mayhem, he kills and then finally he performs a miracle. She spoke better than she knew; for in the burgeoning American potlach of yummy cholesterol, high-priced protein and the infinitely extensible falsie only some sharp delinquency, whether a private needle or a public bomb, seems capable of reminding us that we live perpetually with heaven and hell.

What William S. Burroughs gives us, in his life and his writing, is the example of a deeply committed personality totally uninterested in culture as information, in a surface of "nice" people, in all those time-wasting activities with which even the most earnest hen-track makers seek to beguile the spectre.

Picture a young man brought up in Saint Louis descended from the founder of one of America's great industrial enterprises. The depression reduces the family fortune but by no means completely wipes it out. At Harvard during the first New Deal administration he impresses his contemporaries with the force underlying his political intelligence, his serious studies in poetry and ethnology, his experiments with Yoga. A year or so in corrupting Europe and back to Harvard for graduate study in anthropology.

And now the break. An early traumatic experience has resulted in a rough love life and, even more important, in a loss of confidence in his family. Psychoanalysis removes fear but not a sense of isolation. Self-contrived rejection by the Army after the fall of France strengthens that sense. All of us who failed to participate in the war effort owing to one form of unclubbability or another have, I think, felt the necessity to conduct private wars of our own. Even pacifists and enemy sympathizers participate dialectically; the outsiders feel they need the danger even if they and the purpose find themselves mutually dispensible. In addition Burroughs has the need for commitment, which odd jobs—exterminator, private detective, bartender—cannot give, since a small trust fund effectively excludes him from basic concern. This commitment he finds in addiction to narcotics, an addiction which swallows up his income and gives him a new grim interest in the economy.

However gratifying the sense of urgency and the solidarity of weakness he finds in criminals, their stupidity gets on his nerves. After the war, establishing himself in the vicinity of Columbia University, he becomes a guide, philosopher and the friend of a group of young college boys including Allen Ginsberg and Jack Kerouac, a role he has continued to play for many of us ever since with great success and to our great spiritual profit.

After a period in New Orleans Burroughs heads for Mexico with his wife and two children. There things are possible, living cheaper, dope with less trouble, boys ditto.

At the age of thirty-five, under the prodding of Ginsberg, Burroughs begins writing his first and as yet only published book, *Junky,* an account of his life as an addict in the United States and Mexico, as well as *Queer,* a further account of his Mexican adventures.

After a stay in East Texas helping to run a farm, he accompanies an anthropological expedition through Columbia and visits Peru on a quest for Yage, a drug which induces hallucinations and purportedly endows its users with telepathic powers. Out of this quest comes a series of letters to Ginsberg called *In Quest of Yage,* now a part of his novel, *Naked Lunch.*

Then Tangier, his base of operations from 1954 to the beginning of 1958, when he moves to Paris in search of further psychiatric revelations. This period, given to "steeping himself in vice," to use his own words, is devoted to the composition of *Interzone,* the latest and longest section of *Naked Lunch.* The first part of this period is marked by increasing seclusion, by the horrors of long drawn out and ineffective junk withdrawals and eventually by a cure in England. The second is distinguished by a frenzy of marijuana-stimulated composition and a progressive loosening of ties with Tangier culminating in the definitive move to Paris. Tomorrow India? Greece? Mexico again? Who knows? What we do know is that whatever the scene an incorruptible eye will enjoy its fissures and sustain its strengthlessness.

I first had the good luck to meet Burroughs in New York through Allen Ginsberg just before he sailed for Tangier. At the moment I was at a loose end, housebound out of inertia, unwilling to travel for fear of enrollment in a gaggle of jabbering queens. Meeting this totally autonomous personality gave me the courage to get up off my ass without worrying about what I was conforming or non-conforming to, and I can never thank him enough.

A tall ectomorph—in Tangier—the boys called him *El Hombre Invisible*—his persona constituted by a magic triad of fedora, glasses and raincoat rather than by a face, his first presence is that of a con-man down on his luck. But that impression soon gives way to the feeling that, whatever his luck may be, yours has been very good. A cracker accent and use of jive talk fail to conceal incisive intelligence and a frightening seriousness. "No one owns life," says Burroughs, "but anyone who can pick up a frying pan owns death."

A distinguishing feature is the mania for contacts. One sometimes feels that for him drugs and sex exist only to provide opportunities for making appointments. It is a revealing clue to his tremendous isolation.

He is an indispensable indication that it is possible to be vicious without being slack. How many addicts one knows incapable of more than a sob or a monosyllable, how many queens who seem to have no place in life except the perfume counter at Woolworths or the economy price whorehouse. To use drugs without losing consciousness or articulateness, to love boys without turning into a mindless drab is a form of heroism. With some writers drugs take the place of the excitement of composition; with Burroughs they are rather succedanea for the beatific and malefic visions.

Burroughs' attitude to property is most austere—living quarters tantamount to the worst hotel's worst room and no more personal possessions than what can be packed into a handbag or worn on his back plus a portable typewriter. His motives are partly prudential—one never knows when a spot of bother may render a fast departure mandatory; the less substance involuntarily abandoned, the slighter the pang—and partly self-lacerating; but primarily the renunciation of possessions is the necessary consequence of his non-attachment to inessentials.

Beneath the tics and through the awareness of misery there exist a wholeness and devotedness of pesonality that create repose for Burroughs and instill it in others. I know of no one with whom it is such a delight to share an apartment. Not only awareness, not only psychic generosity, but a calm of spirit that can tame even the most fidgety poltergeist.

Why so much biography in the discussion of a literary figure? First, because of his importance as mentor and example in the lives and works of those writers, Ginsberg and Kerouac particularly, who are trying to recapture American poetry and prose for the total personality. Secondly, because if, as they and I believe, writing is more than a matter of cerebrally selective craftsmanship is, in fact, the total and continuous commitment of a given history, the raw materials of that history have public importance and back up the testimony of that work. And, in the case of Burroughs, the writing is a by-product, however, brilliant, of a force. What I am writing is not only a paean to a writer; it is also a variant of hagiography.

Seen in this light, Burroughs' closest parallel is Genet. His emergence into a sense of reality out of coddled conformity is comparable to Genet's triumph over misery and degradation through consciousness.

Junky is a flat cold narrative interspersed with factual lectures. In the ecological pattern of drug addicts the narrator is reduced to a cipher in the crowd, and the use of the first person is almost a mockery. People's actions and relations only point up the basic isolatedness of each, and the individual's sense of his own existence takes on the bleak unreality of an unloved newspaper paragraph. New York, Lexington Penitentiary, New Orleans and Mexico City pass by in a uniform chill that accurately differentiated topography and characterization somehow make chillier. It is Reisman's lonely crowd with the factitious warmth of convention replaced by the real if forbidding warmth of—junk. But that isn't enough warmth to export;

in fact, the sense of physiological self-sufficiency it imparts blocks all other relations. Meanwhile the tireless lecturer keeps telling us the facts in season and out, medical, legal, anthropological, with an angry impatience. The truth may make you miserable, but it is the truth.

The thirteenth and fourteenth chapters of *Junky* overlap *Queer;* and the thirteenth, particularly, figures a new subjective approach to the theme of isolation. A sick spirit tortures its helpless body to their respective limits. If the isolation of narcotics expresses itself in an aggregate of responseless units, the isolation of homosexuality brings out a unique internality. Bare hard narrative continues in the recitation of environments, of fixes and their sexual equivalents. The conversation, however, is much less clipped than in *Junky* and in the mouth of the narrator turns into a new form, the routine. The first routine in *Queer,* the life and times of the ideal oilman, reveals a double parentage, the lecture and the Tom Sawyer handstand meant to impress the work's *blaue Blume,* Eugene Allerton. Amid the dust and abjection there is a disturbing hint of the atmosphere of the Platonic dialogue told from the point of view of a dispirited Socrates rather than an admiring disciple. The other major routines in the work—a self-lacerating True Confession, the story of Reggie the British agent, the madman's history of chess and the explorer's account of his caravan—are parodies toppling over into outrageousness and are all addressed to Allerton. Only the caravan routine is spoken alone, but it is the outgrowth of an earlier routine to which Allerton refused to go on listening, and in its description of the relations between the explorer and his hired boy menacingly announces the actual trip on which Burroughs takes Allerton in the second half of the book. They go through the Panama and Ecuador formally in search of Yage, but for Burroughs it is the tantalizing but perpetually unsuccessful search for the perfectly spontaneous, perfectly responsive companion. Themes that exfoliate in *Interzone,* particularly the erotic basis of theories of political power, first appear here in a more intimate form: it is the saddest course of *Naked Lunch.*

In *Yage,* Burroughs is alone again. He recounts his travels through the horrors of Panama and much more briefly Ecuador, through the political noxiousness of Colombia, where, as a member of an anthropological expedition, he first tries Yage, through the confined joys of Peru, where life is easy, and he steeps himself in the drug. The actual discovery of the drug plays a relatively small part in the work; at the center are the anthropologist's field report and Burroughs' life in Yage. The formal novelty of the work is expansion of the routines and their independence of an erotic context. Only one has even an imaginary reference to Allerton, the presentation of the relation between a jealous lover and his beloved in terms of a loan company calling on a delinquent debtor. Two others, the death of Billy Bradshinkel, a parody of a slick paper magazine story, and Roosevelt after Inauguration, a violent and obscene account of the imaginary horrors in Washington following the triumph of the New Deal, continue at greater length the pattern of humorous exaggeration established in the routines of *Queer* as does the Zen Routine, in which a Mahatma devoted to what Burroughs likes to call "fact," that is, the maximum consciousness of reality, teases and instructs a disciple too prone to take words for things. The most ambitious routine of all, however, Yage City, is neither parody nor erotic philosophy but a vision of "The Composite City where all the human potentials are spread out in a vast silent market."

And that brings us to *Interzone,* the cold observer in abeyance, the horrid scene and the boisterous routines at the prow. Here, to sketch a progression is pointless, since the work is conceived as a total presence. The various luckless environments come together seeking refuge from unimaginative totalitarianisms that their own maniacally passional selfishness has created. Only the Seven Stages section of Auden's *Age of Anxiety* affords an equal example of "their own disorder as their own punishment."

Hitherto omnipresent "Lee," Burroughs' *nom de guerre,* is here reduced to a sufferer in a hospital and a noncommittal witness to the evils of the County Clerk and the manias of Dr. Benway. Beyond that he fulfills his role as Tiresias, the passive clairvoyant, by disappearing into what he sees. In fact, Lee, the cold if concerned observer, gives way to Dr. Benway, the conscious and impassioned lecturer who shares his patients' weaknesses, as the author's principal mask. Interzone, the superficially bothered resort of individuals on the lam from amalgamation, is over against Freeland, the superficially generous trap for the surrenderers of their individuality, where everything is permitted and nothing ever gets to happen.

The anthropological survey radiates out of Tangier in the Panorama and Market sections of the work. A.J.'s Annual Ball and Hassan's Rumpus Room are expanded routines trembling on the verge of such sheer free fantasy as Voices, which filter to Lee's sickchamber. Islam Inc. provides the political organization and theory that is speeding Interzone toward calamity, first through the presentation of its directorate: A.J. the large extrovert, Hassan the slinky go-between, and Clem and Jody the professionally hateful Americans; and second through the description of the parties of Interzone: the Senders, whose only interest is to exercise power with no thought of its consequences, the Liquefactionists, greedyguts who want to absorb all the richness of all other lives into themselves, the Divisionists, who create ideal responsive friends (see *Queer)* by cutting off bits of their own bodies, and the Factualists, who rejoice in the variety of existence. In this world politics derive from the data of acquaintanceship and romance; only the Factualists are living. Finally, there is Word, in which the author, all masks thrown aside, delivers a long tirade, a blend of confession, routine and fantasy ending in "a vast Moslem muttering."

And now? There are rumors of a work dealing with the night of prehistory. In his last letter to me the author says: "complete dissatisfaction with everything I have done in writing ... Unless writing has the danger and immediacy, the urgency of bullfighting, it is nowhere to my way of thinking ... I am tired of sitting behind the lines with an imperfect recording device receiving inaccurate bulletins ... I must reach the Front."

William S. Burroughs
THE BURROUGHS FILE

The White Subway

UNFINISHED CIGARETTE

The White Subway gathered silent speed as buildings and
landscapes slid by—faster—faster—a blur of film flakes then
pictures leaped into sharp focus—mist and frogs in 1920 roads—
morning sleep of detour—needle beer in Sid's. He was in a long
tunnel of old photos stretching back to his childhood—back—
back—"STOP." The Dutch painter held up his hand "You don't
know what you are doing man. Here's someone to talk to you.
This man knows what he is saying so pay attention to him."

A doctor in a white smock stood by his side: "Now listen
carefully. I can only tell you once. You are coming to a dangerous point. Such a tightrope to walk back across your birth and if
you slip—It is a question of staying right IN THE MIDDLE you
understand." His finger tapped a dial and a needle that oscil-
lated in a narrow band of white light "You must be THERE at
all times. It is like driving a car at full speed over a very bad
road. Be careful of drifting over the hills and far away. Watch
the needle. Keep silence. Keep also tension—engagement. Keep
yourself THERE." His finger tapped the needle "HERE" he
indicated the right side of the dial "is total engagement. You fall
back into body—that is if you are fortunate—Worse things can
happen—and HERE" he indicated the left side of the dial "you
lose yourself—your direction—No this is NOT good to lose the
self before it is yours again—Here I would seem to disagree with
Mr. Gysin—I am no enemy of the little people but their place is
not at the controls of a space craft—certainly not such a crate as
this one—Stay in the middle—Here is your apomorphine
spray—and—oh yes—this button—the laser guns—Never use it
unless you have to. You will know when it is necessary. It should
not be needed at this point—later on—when you reach the blockade." He glanced sharply around, his eyes probing the controls.
"This is a dangerous ship—overloaded with weapons—You will
be lucky if—." He nodded gravely and turned to a dial in his
laboratory. Other birth candidates pressed around him stabbing his vitality centers with black blasts of anti energy—"Keep
silence. Hold in sight—Tension—Engagement." The faces slid

away. Mr. Martin smiles—bits of paper drifting on a St. Louis corner—over the hills and far away—the needle drifting to the left—further further—dirigibles rising from India ink—"Back! Back!" death weakness—His hand moved towards the apomorphine spray—numb—paralyzed—couldn't reach—out of his body through a whirling black funnel—back at the controls now the needle sharp in the middle. Beneath him the 1920s spread a panorama of old films. Cold into radio winds stir the sick dawn. Opium Jones so badly off. Forgotten voices wait for rain. Nitrous flesh swept out "THERE": Dead cigarette smoke—India ink shirt flapping. Knife and blood spreading is written—empty arteries by 1920 pond in a vacant lot. Old friend waves from the cemetery—cold little wind—Some boy from vacant lots dying by 1920 pond—Sid's speakeasy across the flutes.

"Your actors erased poisonous dead world THERE." His finger tapped unfinished cigarette. Ashes fall on Ewyork Onolulu Aris Ome Oston. "And HERE Death takes over the game BEFORE board books. Oh yes—this button—the laser guns: (a black silver sky of broken film.)" Opium sharp focus—iridescent head on needle beer in Sid's speakeasy. He was in a long lane of leaves stretching back to the golf course. Poisonous road shifting elliptically twisted a vast delta of silver paper in the wind across turnstiles and cable cars.

"You will know a young sailor and he said: 'I can only tell you once: led vines and stars back across movements of an old man in mucous of the world. You must be THERE at dank mornings in the school toilet—at full speed over adolescent urinals and far away. Watch from old photos and leaves—tension—engagement—Keep your cobblestone streets and thin boy structures in the middle—Little winds on a St. Louis corner IS total engagement. Nothing HERE'": (indicated the left side of red velvet curtains and rotting teak direction) "'No this does NOT go through the violet sky. Here I see poisonous bones twisted in the mirror—enemy of the little people again—blue light blockade—numb paralyzed earth drained of morning—The needle is dead and see this refuse of opium dens on vacant lots.'"

Other birth candidate rolls a cigarette: "Remember I was abandoned from old movie on the road—empty condom waiting for rain. Nothing can happen on 1920 dial."

Window lighted by the speakeasy—Old friend waves from his cobblestone streets. Adolescent urinals stretch to the postcard sky. "I am dying, Meester? Forgotten in mucous of the world?—"A sweep of wind wipes away many out there—you see—trailing vines a child said as stagnant flowers—bleeding youth—frayed overcoat on a bench—"

Pan plays his flute far away. On the sea wall met a boy image hopping through past time under the ceiling fan—smell of dawn flesh dispersed by little winds—

"Laser guns—the pestilence from board books—necessary—blue light blockade—five times you will be lucky if—" "Dust in the air marks a barrier ended. Remember I was silence to the other birth candidates reaching last cigarette from old movie. No more is written. Over the hills broken books—most ancient face gone far away. The needle is dead. His childhood forgotten refuse behind the billboard. Warm rain in vines from adolescent pedestrians."

World's dead broken film rolls on. Frayed commands filtered last job here. His voice finished. The tour ends at this address. Friend's last flag went down with his reach caught and twisted this blood I created in disaster five thousand years ago—the devious words forever exploded. The soldier's words Mr. Bradly and there is nothing left—dead smoke of the war.

And still as Ahab glided over a sea of night gently accompanied him: "And so, Meester, remember me from galaxies far away? Abandoned before you can wipe away my blood prints?"

Late afternoon shadows a transitory world in his eyes, April held his breath in the presence of dying answer: This sail between worlds for the last time with some sailor's goodbye as I sat there brooding on the old sunlight in his voice when he first picked The Swan pub. He had come, poisonous dream must have seemed so close—blue hand to grasp it. He did not know it was story ended in that late afternoon.

On white steps of the sea wall: "Adios, Meester—into the past. I don't desire face to face meeting."

This twisted dead boy of the new world created in disaster cancels the last and greatest of human dreams. Enchanted movements exploded in the mirror year by year at his touch.

31

Dying this continent. Wonder when he first picked where the story ended?

"Knife and empty arteries. It was a long time ago. Dying blood fingers the flute. Your actors erased, Bradly. Unfinished cigarette here. Head standing on needle beer in Sid's. Last answer from the sea and air of broken film. A long lane of tin types fades into the gold course."

"Remember I was abandoned here long ago—empty waiting on 1920 world in his eyes. Meester forgot the barrier—dying here—disaster cancels little people again—abandoned long ago I don't get out—wind hand trailing coat on a bench, Meester—Friend's last flag, Meester Bradly."

"Ahab, dead flute far away long time ago and there is nothing left."

"Mr. Bradley, precarious guest of my sad galaxies—bleeding into the past on the white steps of Mu—twisted coat on a bench between worlds—empty waiting face gone out—Mr. Bradly, precarious blood whom I created, see this refuse where the story ended."

"Far away adios, Meester—into the past—The white Sabbah cancels this earth—this sail—the new world created in disaster—dead job here—Abandoned coat on a bench—forgotten face—Keep friend's last goodbye, Meester—a child sad as his voice—finished—dust, Meester—caught in story ended—." His finger tapped unfinished cigarette "Meester Bradly you forgot cigarette long ago. Adios marks this address."

"I am dying from a room which slowly fills with heavy blue light. I undressed elliptically in the darkroom. My back was turned to him my coat on a bench. There was a barrier of scraping tin. Dead cigarette smoke in his eyes—precarious broken youth—frayed words, Meester Bradly. Dead birth candidate filtered in his voice—a slow calm answer between worlds: 'dead job here. I bring my brother home. He took some room with another gentleman. It was a long time ago. Last errand since 1859. Told me goodbye in the stale morning filtered with dead cigarette smoke. Remember I am speaking last answer from the sea. Woman from galaxies far away given up the fight. Has extended her sail here. Wipe away my blood prints. Adios Meester.'

"His voice finished. The tour ends. Sabbah as also cancels henceforth this address. Face friend's last answer. The frayed voices couldn't reach. Caught and twisted silence." "Dead boy speaking. Friends THERE in 1859."

"This blood I created in disaster I cancel HERE. Hand far away abandoned film. Have definitely changed lots. The 'reservation' is back from Hell. Sabbah as also cancels the disaster weapons broken twisted in the mirror. Coat on a bench the price you paid. All your words forever exploded at his touch."

Beautiful boy has extended her vines from a sea of night . . . gently tapped the words: "You once, Meester—Remember 'Oh yes goodbye Meester?'—I don't get out on friend's disaster— Standing now against own people."

"Her last blood prints. Like the family changed their plans. His whole presence erased in England. Drew curtains of violet evening in the frayed ship—a knife blade and silence. Transparent mirror enemy is speaking his sail stuck in December abandoned. Voices broken twisted he turns slowly in a whirlpool of silence. Oh yes this price—one rotting ticket. Taken off in near future. Hope you don't mind sharing the trip to England—?"

The year 1859 in Glasgow—Late afternoon shadows on the sea wall met a boy offering ports of the world in his eyes— caught dying answer from a room which slowly fills with blue night. Henceforth this sail between worlds dead. Broken film proffers goodbye and silence. This sad calm answer.

"Twisted dead boy speaking here—poisonous blood I created in disaster. The reservation story ended. Needle is dead at The Swan pub. Light blockade exploded in the mirror."

"Dying galaxies—late, Meester—I don't get out—Blue light blockade. Standing now against own people—Dust marks the spot—Remember I am dying far away—India ink shirt in another race trailing knife blade and silence. Coat on a bench where the story ended." His voice finished. Wind wipes away 'goodbye, Meester.'

Today was like an old,worn-out film being run off—dim, jerky, flickering, full of cuts, and with a plot he could not seize. It was hard to pay attention to it.

Let It Come Down by Paul Bowles Tangier.

From A DISTANT HAND LIFTED

A note on the method used in this text

Since work in progress tentatively titled *a distant hand lifted* consists of walkie-talkie messages between remote posts of interplanetary war the cut up and fold in method here used as a decoding operation. For example agent K9 types out a page of random impressions from whatever is presented to him at the moment : : street sounds, phrases from newspapers or magazine, objects in the room etc. He then folds this page down the middle and places it on another page of tyupewriter messages and where the shift from one text to another is made / marks the spot. The method can approximate walkie-talkie immediacy so that the writer writes in present : : : : remember / my / messages between remote posts of / exploded star / fold in / distant sky / example agent K9 types out a / distant hand lifted / there on / whatever is presented to him / sad boy speaking / from magazine / this page / filtered back "adios" and death / message / from his gun / is / buried in sand / hear this dry / walkie-talkie / plst erased / "You hear now?" / writer writes in present time / drifting / messages / on a windy street / to scan out your message as it were / said / the operation consisting : : : : : : "You are yourself Mr. Bradley Mr. Martin / of course" / who else? / your first arrest wasn't it? / the point is / past time whistling / message that is you / to scan out your message as it were : : : : : : : *'a distant hand lifted'* / : : : : : "You / and I / sad old / broken film / knife / cough / it lands in / cough / present time / long cough / decoding arrest / wasn't it?" : : : : : : cough / immediacy / cough / empty arteries must tell you / cough / 'adios' / who else? / cough / drew Sept 17, 1899 over New York???

Mr. Bradley Mr. Martin stood there after / the order to drop the atom bomb / wasn't anything to say / housekeeper makes a statement / : "hollow / still East Texas afternoon / fried fragments / I wiped away vapor / looking through the smoke /"

"no feelings / may I venture? / that's *your* Martin / irrevocably committed to / a long / existence / So called / the necessary / uh fabrication organism/to interfere/:we of the nova police/"

"was a boy / I own cops out of Hell / all the Grey Guards" / said Martin softly / a faint odor of / nova / in the air / as it were / summoned / his saddle / uh belated / there / in / cigarette smoke drifting / no more / peg to hang it on / like where? / "Well, Martin I / tell you just where / I start / : the uh 'public' cooling system under / survey. /"

"That's mighty close, Clem / well / I / closed down./"

"may I venture / 'Big Red' / because you had no choice? that your / old signal / irrevocably committed to / uh rather special / uh cooling system / : *sizzling there naked that young officer?????????* "I start blind / had no choice / that / pinpoint / existence / sizzling / rays of negation and death / only exist / after the fact of nova" / "Haven't you forgotten / some / harder names / back from Hell? / put down / plain Mr. Jones / or Mr. J / if you prefer / the Inferential Kid / exploded the / uh 'public' cooling system / there in / cigarette smoke drifting / grey ash of Pluto / blown from / empty sleeve / which is precisely how my / uh presence is / uh belatedly / infered / you??? / *officer ???* /precisely / to use / soiled clothes / of / fabrication organism??? / appears / necessary / to / uh flash you the grey / nova / police / lack of you / may infer / belated / a little smarter / clutch / your / parenthetically dying / fingernail of Nagasaki / light system / Martin / "

"And parenthetically / in all this / my name was / 'Fried Fragments'/ ??? Well? Martin? / Just / no / trials in human beings / you can look any place / they all went away / no good / no bueno / clom Fliday /" "Big Red? / please / remember / there naked / that / young / officer / special / uh flash you understand / from / special / uh / police / no / more / peg / to / hang / it / on / Martin / and parenthetically / a gun / defined / the statement. / 'Big / 'Red' / you are / no / where / you / left / there / naked / that / young / officer / because / you / had no choice? / that forgotten / boy / cops out / his existence /

sizzling / to / nova???????? nova police / sizzling to interfere /
in such pain / as it were / summoned / a lot of / harder names /
haven't you forgotten / some / boy / own / cops / out of Hell /
now ? Add it all / up now / against harder names / from / uh
special police / uh / literally / uh / sizzling / parenthetically /
to interfere. / a young cop drew the curtains.

"nova heat bugging all of us. You know how laws are. Once
they start asking questions there's no end to it?????????? Few
things in my own past I'd just as soon forget."

"You / left / there / naked / that young / officer / *because you
had no choice?????????* *here* / Ring those screaming fragments
: : : : : : : : / "Mr. Bradly / I / *here* / *burning* / *burning* / rockets
across the valley / *whole sky burning*" You call that young
officer "Operation Expendable??????? Servants who did what
you were afraid to do yourself just so many bangs of heavy
metal junk???????? / "Medics broke out 'the boy who paid' and
we all took a shot" / "I may venture that / the / uh / 'fireworks'
/ the / uh / 'public cooling system'????????" "My confessions
have finished off three hardened police inspectors remember????????? / memory hit the old detective like a knife / "God /
I remember" / (who else? / your first arrest wasn't it?) Just old
moonshiners you might say setting on our dead heavy metal
ass condensing the cold heavy silver water of exploding stars.
dry county you understand / you hear that dry desert? / Just as
cool *there* as it is hot *here.* A word to the wise guy : : : : : : : : : / buy
a Martin Frigidaire /

"Keep the home fires burning because they burn cool blue to me
/ you remember me? Honest Mart The Working Man's Friend?
I pushed the best cap in / New Orleans used to cap it in those
days remember? Later it was all packs and a nickle cap strictly
from milk sugar, You going to miss me honey / old friend you
know / the oldest / A chorus of sincere homosexual football
coaches sing: "In the sweet bye and bye" / An old junkie selling
Christmas seals on North Clark Street / "Fight tuberculosis,
folks / cough / lake wind hit the old junkie like a knife / The
Priest they called him / just an old friend left / between worlds.

"Should auld acquaintance be forgot and never brought to
mind??????"

We'll take a cup of kindness yet for the sake of auld lang syne /
/ / / Bradly stands there in the empty ballroom / "after the ball
is over" / under streamers of cold grey ash

"What an old corn ball. Just hope he can drag it out till I get my
bags packed. Oh, don't bother with all that junk, John. John
this is *nova heat.*"

"Hell, Arch, / message from boy's magazine / drew iron tears
down Pluto's cheek. I don't like welchers, Martin. You pulled an
oven in the wrong company. Chilie house it all up Martin and
laugh out a few more cobblestone streets" / And since you not
always remember ash blown from my sleeve was war and
death / Bradly's broken junk of exploded star / twilight train
whistles in a distant sky / cigarette smoke drifting far away
and long ago / a distant hand lifted / there on a windy street /
half buried in sand / sad calm boy speaking here on the farthest shore / dead stars splash his cheekbone with silver ash / a
transitory magazine filtered back 'adios' and death / The soldier? / to him my question???? from his gun distant smoke /
from his gun a dusty answer / half buried in sand / hear this
dry desert blockade exploded / last gun-post erased / You hear
now that hideous electric / whisper of / last young officer /
naked / there / screaming / hand lifted / *for you ????????* Blood
I created paid? Martin / clear as the white hot sky / *Don't ever
call me again, Martin*" /

Mr. Bradly Mr. Martin said / the empty room said / the
cigarette smoke behind him said / : : : : : : : "You are yourself Mr.
Bradly Mr. Martin who never existed at all / Who else? Your
first arrest wasn't it? Well remember a young cop walking
down past time whistling "Annie Laurie" twirling his club drew
Sept 17, 1899 over New York.

ash / streaking his cheekbones / on the face / "Klinker is dead
/ Major Ash is dead." / a silver adios from / this shattered /
grey hand / brought / train whistles to a distant / window /
tracks / half buried in sand / on lonely sidings / blurred / boy
speaking here / a million / dead stars splash his cheekbones /
like flint sparks / "18" he said / waiting / in the clinic / on / the
name / Honest Mart / far away pushed the best cap in New

37

Orleans / hands shaking / a blackened spoon / remember? / 'state of vision' he said / in oriental eyes / a cruel unreasoning hate / you, writer / yes, I can hear you / might close / the soldier's words / like a knife / feeling for / a distant / cough / spitting blood / on white steps of the sea wall / wounded street boy / must tell you / and I / sad old / broken film / giving you my / toy soldiers / put away / in the haunted attic / see this refuse / Bradly's broken junk of exploded star / far away / a blackened gun / half buried in sand / You may infer / my / typewriter / and so / there on / sad old tunes / sad old showmen / peanuts / in 1920 movie / you may infer / books and toys / put away / in the past / waiting the touch / of a distant hand / half-buried in sand / twisted coat on a bench / cough / a trail of blood down white steps of the sea wall / knife and empty arteries / must tell you / : : : : : "You are yourself 'Mr. Bradly Mr. Martin' / cough / who else? / cough / trailing knife / cough / it lands in an alley / cough / the sea ahead / cough / way long / cough / steps few / cough / Twisted / falls / remember? / your first arrest wasn't it? / : : : : : : you never existed at all / He could not choose his own place where the story ended / the appropriate button / past time whistling 'Annie Laurie' / Sept. 17, 1899 over New York / a distant hand lifted.

THE CONSPIRACY

I took the subway up to 116 Street and walked across the Columbia campus to Mary's flat. Why didn't I think of her first? A university campus... the perfect hideout... And I could count on Mary, count on her 100 per cent... The building was a four-story brownstone. The windows shone clean and black in the morning sunlight. I walked up three flights and knocked on the door. Mary opened it and stood there looking at me.

"Come in," she said, her face lighting up. "Want a cup of coffee?" I sat down with her at the kitchen table and drank coffee and ate a piece of coffee cake.

"Mary, I want to hide out here for a while... I don't know how long exactly... You can say someone rented the extra room to write his thesis. He doesn't want to go out of the room or see anyone til it's finished... You have to buy his food and bring it to him... He's paying you 100 dollars to stay there three weeks or however long it takes... I just killed two detectives."

Mary lit a cigarette: "Hold-up?"

"No. It's much more complicated than that. Let's move to the room in case somebody comes. I'll tell you about it.

"Light junk sickness, when I wake up needing a shot, always gives me a sharp feeling of nostalgia, like train whistles, piano music down a city street, burning leaves ... I mentioned this to you, didn't I?"

Mary nodded, "Several times."

"An experience we think of as fleeting, incalculable, coming and going in response to unknown factors. But the feeling appears without fail, in response to a definite metabolic setup. It's possible to find out exactly what that setup is and reproduce it at will, given sufficient knowledge of the factors involved. Conversely it is possible to eliminate nostalgia, to occlude the whole dreaming, symbolizing faculty."

"And you mean it's been done?"

"Exactly. Scientists have perfected the anti-dream drug, which is, logically, a synthetic variation on the junk theme ... And the drug is habit-forming to a point where one injection can cause lifelong addiction. If the addict doesn't get his shot every eight hours he dies in convulsions of oversensitivity."

"Like nerve gas."

"Similar ... In short, once you are hooked on the anti-dream drug you can't get back. Withdrawal symptoms are fatal. Users are dependent on the supply for their lives and at the same time, the source of resistance, contact with the myth that gives each man the ability to live alone and unites him with all other life, this is cut off. He becomes an automaton, an interchangeable quantity in the political and economic equation."

"Is there an antidote?"

"Yes. More than that, there is a drug that increases the symbolizing faculty. It's a synthetic variation of telepathine or yageina, the active principle of Bannisteria Caapi."

"And where do you come in?" Mary asked.

"Five years ago I made a study of Bannisteria Caapi, the Indians call it Yage, Ayanhuaska, Pilde, in South America, and found out something about the possible synthetic variations. The symbolizing or artistic faculty that some people are born with—though almost everyone has it to some degree as a child—can be increased a hundred times. We can all be artists infinitely greater than Shakespeare or Beethoven or Michelangelo. Because this is possible, the opposite is also possible. We can be deprived of symbol-making power, a whole dimension excised, reduced to completely rational, non-symbolizing creatures ... Perhaps ...

"Yes?"

"I was wondering whether ... Well ... let it go. We have enough to think about."

That afternoon Mary went out and bought the papers. There was no mention of Hauser and O'Brien.

"When they can keep that quiet they must have a fix in near the top. With the ordinary apparatus of law looking for me I might have one chance in a hundred.... This way ... "

I told Mary to go to a pay phone in Times Square, call police headquarters, and ask for Hauser. Then go across the street and see what happens. She was back in half an hour.

"Well?"

She nodded. "They stalled me, said to hang on a minute, he was on the way. So I cut across the street. Not more than three minutes later a car was there. Not a police car.They blocked both entrances to the drug store—two went in and checked the phone booths. I could see them questioning the clerk, and he was saying in pantomime: 'How should I know? A thousand people in and out of here every day!'"

"And now you're convinced I'm not having a pipe dream? I wish I could have one . . . Haven't seen any gum in a dog's age . . . "

"So what do we do now?"

"I don't know. I'd better start at the beginning and bring you up to date."

What was the beginning? Since early youth I had been searching for some secret, some key with which I could gain access to basic knowledge, answer some of the fundmental questions. I found it difficult to define. I would follow a trail of clues. For example, the pleasure of drugs to the addict is relief from the state of drug need. Perhaps all pleasure is relief and could be expressed by a basic formula. Pleasure must be proportioned to the discomfort or tension from which it is the relief. This holds for the pleasure of junk. You never know what pleasure is until you are really junk sick. Drug addiction is pehaps a basic formula for pleasure and for life itself. That is why the habit, once contracted, is so difficult to break, and why it leaves, when broken, sucks a vacuum behind. (A slip but what a succinct expression of the oral basis of addiction, the horror of oral deprivation of "sucking a vacuum.") The addict has glimpsed the formula, the bare bones of life, and this knowledge has destroyed for him the ordinary sources of satisfaction that make life endurable. To go a step further, to find out exactly what tension is, and what a relief, to discover the means of manipulating these factors . . . The final key always eluded me, and I decided that my search was as sterile as the alchemist's search for the philosopher's stone. I decided that it was an error to think in terms of some secret or key or formula . . . The secret is that there is no secret . . . But I was wrong. There is a secret now in the hands of ignorant and evil men. A

secret beside which the atom bomb is a noisy toy . . . And like it
or not I was involved . . . I had already ante-ed my life . . . I had
no choice but to sit the hand out.

THE CUT

Some day later Johnny's face fragments of Yen let out his
"Oh there's my doctor," in liquid gurgles through his Broad
Accident.

"You'll love him talked life jelly. It sticks and the doctor
grows on you like Johnny."

His soft boneless head tissue was imbedded in the doctor's
right side. His scalpel out of Johnny's ear trim where they move
like: "Doctor, I want you a slow green juice. And he's a fellow
over the other. Some time he don't hardly ass." The waiter
turned with a technical grin. Melodious little bird cry? "Jelly?"
Over each to here covered with grey-green fuzz. The Doctor
pulled ace an inch higher, trimmed the papillas around a dead
cold cold undersea eye exuded my friend Mr. D the Agent
Hydraulic pressure the doctor's left lip. Flesh was dreamy and
innocent. The Doc inside was a cold tentacle, hear what you are
saying. He pulled his Abbreviated Fibrous and wrote the bill on
instruments. Two ambulanace attendants seized the Waiter.
He jerked free and ran for the door. The doctor threw a stetho-
scope that wrapped around the waiter's legs like a bolo. He fell
with a cry of despair and the attendants carried out his empty
body. The doctor got slowly up on long stalk legs; he supported
himself on two flexible canes.

When the wind is right you can hear them scream in The
Town Hall Square. And everybody says, "But this is
interesting."

THE DANISH OPERATION

The doctor was sitting in a surgical chair of gleaming nickel. His soft boneless head was covered with grey fuzz, the right side of his face an inch lower than the left side swollen smooth as a boil around dead, cold undersea eye.

"Doctor, I want you to meet my friend Mister D The Agent, and he's a lovely fellow too."

An uncertain smile flickered the doctor's left lip. His left eye embedded in pink coral flesh was dreamy and innocent. The right eye touched D inside with cold familiar tentacle.

"Sometimes he don't hardly hear what you are saying. He's very technical."

The doctor reached out his abbreviated fibrous fingers in which surgical instruments caught neon and cut Johnny's face into fragments of light. "Jelly," the Doctor said, liquid gurgles thru his hardened purple gums. His tongue was split and the two sections curled over each other as he talked: "Life jelly. It sticks and grows on you like Johnny."

Little papules of tissue were embedded in the doctor's hands. The doctor pulled a scalpel out of Johnny's ear and trimmed the papules into an ashtray where they stirred slowly exuding a green juice. The doctor crossed one leg over the other with a slow hydraulic pressure. Thick black hair suddenly sprouted from his ankles disintegrated his sock to black wool dust. The doctor goosed a young waiter and the scalpel disappeared up his ass. He pulled an indelible pencil from the waiter's fly and signed his bill on the waiter's cuff "as you say."

ANCIENT FACE GONE OUT

Inspector J. Lee of the Nova Police: "Mr. I & I Martin turned out to be very small potatoes indeed, to be in fact exactly what he appeared to be: a broken down vaudeville actor on the heavy metal. Obviously this mind could not even think in Nova terms. He did, however, have the courage to give us at least one of the basic identities of Mr. D. The man he named was a doctor, a psychiatrist. As always he had the most impeccable references. He was opposed to shock therapy, lobotomy, forcible confinement. "The free will," he said, "is never destructive." Quite a statement when you come to think about it. At first the doctor blandly and humorously denied any connection with the Nova Mob. But faced by Mr. Martin, trailing thousands of other informants in his wake like the Pied Piper, a vast squealing host, all in a state of unbelievable terror (in all my experience as a police officer I have never witnessed such total terror), all asking our protection on absolutely any terms, and all fingered the doctor as *the* Mr. D, the man who gave the orders. Mr. D, also known as Great Amber Clutch, also known as Iron Claws ... No the doctor did not "break down and confess." Iron cool he sat down and stated that he had indeed given the order to drop atom bombs on Hiroshima and Nagasaki as the first step in his Nova plan.

"Mr. D, would you care to make a statement?"

"A *statement.* Any 'statement' I might make would be meaningless to you who cannot think in terms of white hot gas, nebulae, light years and anti-matter. Your technicians can write the formulae I dictate but they cannot *think* in these terms. My statement, if complete, would be incomprehensible."

"Please make an attempt, Mr. D."

"Very well but if you are to understand even partially you must suspend all human feelings and value judgements. Your so-called feelings are not relevant here. I don't feel. I think. And all my thinking is directed towards Nova. Why? you ask. Why? Why? Why? There is no why. Understand this: *I have no motives.* I act appropriately and automatically. And all my automatically appropriate actions extending through millions of minds and bodies are precisely directed towards Nova. The man, the so-called doctor, sitting here simply happens to be the most suitable brain I could use. That is, he carries out my orders without any emotional static or distortion. Once the atom bombs were dropped I had the necessary pain photos to stop anyone who considered to interfere. Nova was in machine terms inevitable on planet earth.

Now a few basic principles: Any word, any image is defined, that is precisely shaped like wax in a mould by what it is not. I am the mould. I am at all times precisely what you are not. So every movement every thought every word or picture must have my shape. You live in a mould and I am that mould. Image *is* organism. Any form of life with an image whether human or nonhuman is an organism. Now consider the limits of what you call organic life. Narrow limits. Temperature—(Believe me this is the most important. Key image of heat under all my power)—Water. Sustenance. Oxygen. You can of course easily conceive organisms with wider limits, built to endure higher or lower temperatures, breathe different gases, eat different food, and such organisms exist, millions of them. Once I start the proliferation of image there is only one end to that. Now all organisms are by definition *limited* and precisely defined by what they are not. And I am what all organisms are not. I only exist where no organism is. I only exist where no life is. I only exist where you are not. Mr. Gysin speaks of rubbing out the word and the image. Why do I oppose this? The answer comes before the question. I *am* opposition. The opposition that defines all organism. And let me take this opportunity of replying to my creeping, sniveling, organismic opponents on this world or any other. I am not a parasite. You do not give me anything I need. I need nothing. I need zero. Parasites are organisms I use. Such parasite organisms are of course basic to the Nova formulae. Actually the Nova formulae *is* number. Image *is* time. Time is radioactive. Take your own planet. Now let us say I heat up the mould that surrounds you. I heat it up to a point where you cannot exist. I squeeze the mould tighter and tighter. SPUT. The mould explodes in a white hot blast. The mould now contains nothing. I am."

"Mr. D, may I uh venture to say that what you have just told

45

us, interesting and uh enlightening as it may at first appear, is not altogether convincing? You begin by telling us we will not understand your uh statement, go on to make a statement that I for one found quite understandable in the course of which, however, you uh indulge in what can only be described as uh fabrications quite as blatant as the uh fabrications I detected in the statement of Mr. Martin. The uh misrepresentations of Mr. Martin are now quite obvious as the uh maneuvers of an uh poker player. He pretended to be the leader of the Nova Mob, indulged in uh wildly provocative behavior, his uh mighty half nelson descending again and again with carefully contrived awkwardness spelling out of course: 'SOS. For God's sake come and get me!' In short Mr. Martin summoned the Nova Police. He was not stupid enough to believe your promises. Nor did we of the Nova Police believe for a moment that Martin actually was the leader of the Nova Mob though we pretended to believe this.

"May I venture to suggest, doctor, at the risk of wounding your uh pride that perhaps somewhat the same situation obtains in your case as in the case of Mr. Martin? That is to say an uh difficult and not in all respects satisfactory uh interpersonal relationship between Doctor R and Mr. uh D? You say you oppose Mr. Gysin because you *are* opposition? I cannot speak for my uh colleagues in the department but I for one find this answer not in all respects candid or complete. May I suggest that you opposed Mr. Gysin because you had no choice? That you were irrevocably committed to, in fact I might say addicted to, the uh orders of Mr. D? That you are in fact even more of an addict than Mr. Martin? That you are, if I may be allowed to mould a phrase, an 'orders addict?' And may I suggest further that your uh statement is incomplete because you do not *know* the answers? We know that Mr. D never told any of his agents any more than the uh minimum consistent with the uh performance of their uh duties and that this Minimum Information—M.I.—was expressed in mathematical formulae. We know that Mr. D lied to all his agents. I suggest that he also lied to you, doctor. I suggest further that you are not *the* Mr. D. That *the* Mr. D. in fact does not exist but is simply the uh hypothetical quantity at the end of an infinite series of which you and Mr. Martin are actually the uh lower integers. "I uh must apologize Mr. uh D if *my* statement or rather should we say the uh colorless question of an uh rather special police officer is uh meaningless to a being of your uh seemingly irrevocable commitments. I am uh unaccustomed to formulate in uh verbal terms or any other and my uh performance is therefore unrehearsed and I do not propose to uh offer an uh repeat performance."

"Ahab, last flag flaps on appropriate actions extending through Board Books. The past is refuse precisely directed. Wind past remote doctor sitting here. Simply happens the Yankee brain I could use. He has a long and ancient face gone out. He is now without motives trailing vines in mucous of the world. Without any emotional static answers your summons. Bombs were dropped and I had the necessary broken books to interfere. Nova was fading and silence to planet earth adrift in sunlight before body. He could not order his own place where the story ended, the appropriate button. Henceforth to interrogate him he knows is written. It was not necessary to tell him. Understood in any case."

JUST SO LONG AND LONG ENOUGH

Suppose image is outlined by word flowers in his head just so long and long enough under white hot skies—Without innoculation—(forgetting me remember me)—laid him down paralyzed by virus enemy a hopeless case—We know you are back—Thing happens that can't be done—looked at dog-proof room—met women of Venus face to face—We doctors know the compromise of dual universe—After April that ground will not take May—Oh say can you see people come and go and are no more—Last boy speaking:

"They stamped 'paid' on my man from the Argentine—One tropical tramp—Old man sits in a cafe smiling today's cigarette is a Bristol—Lydia E. deficiency you know—Who would water and serve?—A young clerk and what of it we should worry declared himself The Angel Of Death—(and death I think is no parenthesis)—Nervous system incapable of thinking was all by the original colonists—He reflected that the actual consignment arrived in Finland—Buffalo Bill's out of the biologic film justlikethat—Jesus he was a handsome arrival—Do you see life declined?—The police established that or this—(Every language even deafanddumb removed to parenthesis)—My sweet, fold etcetera to bed—The technical department is like a perhaps hand to start to hesitate to stop faulty equipment—And three faces had been pointedly ignored.

Eddieandbill came running from the past—Suitcase for storage—Tomorrow will not be too late—Reaped their sowing and 'vent in cigarette smoke—Flotsam and jetsam on dawn flesh—Sleep well—Invisible stars and enough—

"Young death, you who are silent, do you see life?—Stood on a corner there or here that or this—Even after April he looked for May—Oh say can you see by the dawn's noose a Negro—(stagnant parenthesis)—My sweet old etcetera stands by the turnstile—Yes is a pleasant country:

"How do you like your blue eyed boy with dead flesh, 1920 shirt flapping in the lost lands?—(suppose Puerto Assis)—Young ways of silence held between his thumb—Do you see life?—Sad movie drifting in that or this—Brief boy on screen just so long and long enough, perhaps hand broken, fading— Oh say can you see the dawn break centuries come and go and are no more—Last answer echoes on ending earth—I say to you now vacant film—Your lover turned left on Madison Avenue, went in and changed a dollar—We doctors know he picked up a hell of a good universe next to Grand Central—Defunct who used to ride the junk meet slide onetwothreefour into the past— Mister Death it may not always be Mister Martin—Smiling out into space I say to you hollow name—No longer any shelter in there or here that or this—Last 1920 film for Death is beside you—Go now through muslin billboards—Just so long and long enough a vibrating static gun writes—Mister Martin, the world answers your summons no more—Stranger face and onetwothreefour silence—I say to you be gone, Ahab—Last flag flaps there or here—A child sorrowful as my country will go pulling all the sky—Thing happens that can't be done—I say to you cross the dead sky flesh here or there—Adios of Saturn—Sleep well—Empty room justlikethat—Nothing here now—Stone silence of ending earth."

WHO IS THE THIRD THAT WALKS BESIDE YOU

"Now it might surprise you to know there was another man in your position some thirty-five years ago today" his voice trails off. The ash gathers on his Havana held in a delicate grey cone the way it does on a really expensive cigar. "Yes, he wanted to give it all back, everything he's ever taken anywhere. Oh he'd walk down the street giving a smile back here, a gracious nod over there, and a firm young ass over *here* (stay in line Gertie). He'd breathe life and sweetness back into bones rotten with strontium and even understandably top secret 'Operation Pee Pee', the bones and blood and brains of a hundred million more or less gooks down the drain in green cancer piss, would be reversed. Tomorrow when he was properly rested he would have a talk first with his bankers and later of course with Winkhorst in the Technical department to set 'Operation Rewrite' going round the clock" ("/laser guns washing *in present time*/rockets across the valley / whole sky burning / ". His sad servant stands on the burning buckling deck of an exploding star, last glimpse through gun smoke in

"Remember when you were a kid and Relative Albert was just writing two plus two equals nova on the blackboard and you told the other boys if you were ten light years away you would be able to see your birthplace and yourself as a baby? Well, it's all out there, the refuse of all past time on earth worked flints empty condoms needle beer in Sid's all the old names. They want to eat and they want to eat regular because they are trapped in image and image is an eating virus. Now you understand about time? After a certain point you can't go on feeding the past; too much past and not enough present because 'present time' *is* the point where the image virus of past time finds traction in present host. So the host walks out on the past, he walks out on the present *pre* sent at the same time you got the point now you dumb hick the intersection point in the urinal of present time? Well it's all urine and about time to retire. Some things I find myself doing I'll just pack in is all. Now look, this whole time thing, past image feeding on the present, we knew it had to end some time but remember

"Who is the third that walks beside you? The third column of time? Some wise guy come around to your own people with these 1920 scraps? *Have been in desperate battle.* We want to hear pay talk Daddy, and we want to hear pay talk *now.*"

"So those mutinous troops broke into the beautybanks of time and distributed our personal exquisitries to the bloody apes before they could go and get physical and all sort a awful contest pile up like a Most Graceful Movement Contest and a registered junky could hardly get through to Boot's for the fag ballet dancers leaping about. All of us looking about for some refuge maybe some evil old bitch at least in a kiosk spitting the black stuff cold and heavy but when we go to connect she is a "Sweet Old Flower Lady" get a fix of her. "Kiosk Kate" can wilt and sag the croissant on your plate " / I saw it move I tell you / " two hundred yard range if the wind is right is now a "Sweet Old Flower Lady" pim-pam just like that a filthy shambles why "Gracious Waiter Day" up-called a pestilent cloud of singing waiters from the streets of war and death long ago and far away. You see, Mr. Bradly, that boy was your servant who did what you were afraid to do yourself and you laughed at him for doing it and joked about Operation Expendable in the urinals of present time.)

" / In fact that man had always experienced difficulty in dealing with his social inferiors. Like now standing in the shop, his casting rod and fishing plug slung over open shoulder, trying with the most lamentable results to impersonate a barefoot boy with his string of bull-heads, or is it just plain old country bull-shit from a Saturday Evening Post cover? He twisted rapidly, scooping up the change like a boy who has just heard 'last one in is a sissy' and maladroitly snagged an old peasant in the scrotum with his fishing plug. Then in a mistimed attempt at easy joviality he snapped open his Hollywood switch blade and said: "Well I guess we'll just have to cut the whole thing off." He muttered something about calling a doctor, made a vague ineffectual gesture from a *New Yorker* cartoon inadvertently blinding the proprietor's infant son. Finding that all his overtures of goodwill had fallen quite flat he ran back to the 1920's where he took refuge when you were on the junk yourself sure you knew you had to kick *some* time but you said: "Premature. Premature. Give me a little more junk a little more time." Time *is* junk. Junk is time moving at the speed of light. You remember the first few shots before you are hooked again the speed-kick flashing through 1920 streets in a fast car but you can't see the car just the old warehouses and cobblestone streets rushing past you in a silent river of past time? When you take a shot you are in the time-film moving back in time at the speed of light. Now look, a blast does not move at the speed of light but light from the blast does. You understand now? We are staying ahead of the blast in our image moving at the speed of light. Oh say can you see exploding star *here* / 'blighted finger-tips unfinished cigarette' / Look any place. Breathe the lack of vagrant ball players. Breathe? Well, like you say: nothing nothing. You see now what you breathe you dumb hick? You breathe in Paco Joselito Henrique; in their soiled clothes in their soccer scores in their dusty flesh. Flash of bombs must tell you in their eyes? I am the Director. You have known me for a long time. 'Mister, leave cigarette money.' Sad muttering street boy voices on the pontine marshes can the Cutest Old Clochard be far behind? Perhaps the most distasteful thing was the Benevolent Presence Contest in the course which "Sad Poison Nice Guy" irradiated the galaxy right into a taffy-pull of the sweet sick stuff and the citizens still belching it out two weeks later.

Well every whistle-stop had its Quality Champ and you know who wins a quality contest because he includes the other contestants in or out as the case may be the winner stands there in the empty ring . . . and Final Quality Day when all the winners of local and specialized contests met in a vast arena . . . scarcely a man is now alive . . . just one shot that's all it took . . . don't ask me who won because I wasn't *there*. / "

" / You may infer his absence by that ⌐r this in exactly the same relation as before the contest he retroactively did not take part in. "The Not There Kid" was not *there*, empty turnstile marks the spot. So disinterest yourself in my words. Disinterest yourself in anybody's words, In the beginning was the word and the word was bull-shit. Yes sir, boys, it's hard to stop that old writing arm more of a habit than using. Been writing these RX's five hundred thousand years in Sid's, soothing his shattered nerves with long cool draughts of needle beer. All the old tunes and sad old showmen stand there in blue twilight Silver Dollar Dan and Little Boy Blue dead stars fading sad train whistles a distant sky. / "

" / Stranger, forget seventy tons to the square inch and be gone at the flutes. Death takes over in busy lands ashes gutted cities of America and Europe. Empty air marks authority over all antagonists late afternoon on white steps of the set. See, the chains are fallen. Long long radio silence on Portland Place. Light years of youth flapping down a windy street with the torn September sky."

white steps:

"You come with me Meester?"

"J's words once. Yes all the words were mine once. You heard in this Morocco night last voices hopelessly calling. Come closer smell of blood and excrement communicate directly.

Good-bye Mister. I must go. *The tide is coming in at Hiroshima.* Exploded star between us."

and sure hate to pack you boys in with a burning-down word habit. But I am of course guided by my medical ethics and the uh intervention of The Board of Health no more *no mas*. My writing arm is paralyzed ash, blown from an empty sleeve do our work and go. / "

Here comes the old knife-sharpener in lemon sun, light blue eyes reflected from a thin blade, blood on white steps of the sea-wall, afternoon shadow in dying eyes. "Good-bye, Mister. Get off the point. It is precisely time. It's you who have assembled from the broken streets of war and death the burning buckling deck of an exploding star. With wind and dust good-bye."

THE LAST POST *DANGER AHEAD*

Fort Charles
Sunday, September 17, 1899

A silent Sunday to the post our flag at half mast
against tall black windows of the dormitory a distant voice so painful to scan out: ' / Enemy inter-

"Last glimpse of a sad toy army paid all our
strength click of distant heels over the hills and
far away remember ' / Laser gun *washing in present*

Wasn't anything to say. "Mr. Bradly Mr. Martin" stood
there on dead stars heavy with his dusty answer drew
September 17, 1899 over New York that morning giving

cepted September 17, 1899 over New York' Klinker is
dead I knew him. Had no luck. Whistling 'Annie Laurie'
against the frayed stars laser guns washing a sad toy

time rockets across the valley / *whole sky burning* /'
This sad stranger never called retreat, Mister"
torn sky in the ashen water frayed stars of youth

you my toy soldiers put away steps trailing a lonely
dining room world I created quite empty now light
years of youth flapping down a windy street with the

soldier down a postcard road books and toys put away
bare feet twisted on a fence there by the creek
empty as his sad old tune 'that n'er forgot will be'

there across the playground against tall black windows
of the dormitory last glimpse of a sad toy hand lifted
far away : : 'Goodbye, Mister. I have opened the gates

torn September sky' / Have I done the job here? Will
he hear it? / ' stump of an arm dripping stars across
the golf course smell of sickness in the room these

telling you clear as the old sunlight over New York
'Enemy intercepted.'   " / telling me / laser guns
washing egg nog' running two strainers closed down

for you" twisted coat on a bench—barely audible
click: a distant voice so painful stopped in Johnny's
mind a distant hand fell from his shoulder just

foreign suburbs here cool remote Sunday telling you
boy soldier never called retreat frayed sizzling a
distant hand fell here laser guns washing light ye-

"Cobble Stone Cody / Any second now the whole fucking
shit house goes up / Any-post-shit birds, let's see
your arms / burning stump of mine just telling you c-

telling you a soldier spit blood for you here across
the valley clear as the luminous sky our flag is still
there a transitory magazine must tell you the

-ars over New York Little Boy Blue paid on the table
far away never came out that afternoon at recess
time I watched the torn sky bend with the wind

lear as the sky 'enemy intercepted over New York'
So, Mister, remember me there on a windy street half
buried in sand / "   Sad calm boy speaking

price in smoke. We can break radio silence now 'Annie
Laurie' was a code tune just enemy intercepted
September 17, 1899 over New York the Piper pulled

stars splash the silver answer back on lost youth
there books and toys trailing blood down windy steps
far away smell of ashes rising from the typewriter

here on the shore dead stars splash his cheek bone
with silver ash. This is fore you distant hand lifted
on a dead star Klinker is dead. A sad toy soldier

down the sky. Now he didn't go a-looking for to show
you the papers clear as 'Annie Laurie.' For half a
line no repeat performance in *any* naborhood. Last

a black silver star of broken film rockets across
the valley all the light left on a star drifting away
down a windy street forever adios from this ad-

steps from the lake from the hill from the sky.
Rockets fell here on these foreign suburbs*******
****

gun post erased in a small town newspaper*********
****
****

dress of blood and excrement. The cabin reeks of
exploded star.***********************************
****

You can watch our worn out
film dim jerky far away
shut a bureau drawer *****

PALM SUNDAY TAPE

(TORNADO DEAD 223 NEW YORK POST)

Monday, April 12, 1965

The Palm Sunday Tape was prepared like this: A week before Palm Sunday I had recorded on my Wollensack a symphony by a Soviet composer if my memory serves and some radio short wave static—(most interesting sound on the air)—In the course of the week I would run the tape from time to time without playing or recording just wind forward or back you understand just stopping at random to cut in short sections of text. Where I cut in of course the music or static and later the words were wiped off the tape creating new juxtapositions. I cut in sections from *Some of Your Blood* by Theodore Sturgeon—A high school magazine called *Excelsior* edited by Alan Berger— *Horde* Magazine edited by Johnny Byrne, Lee Harwood, Roger Jones & Miles, No. 1, December, 1964—pieces of Pete Brown, Michel Couturier, L.M. Herrickson, George Dowden, Spike Hawkins, Lee Harwood, Miles, Neil Oram—*The Day Jesse James was Killed* by Carl W. Breihan (April 3, 1881)—and some texts of my own ... So you understand when Palm Sunday rolled around there was already quite some layers of cut tape on the machine. Well it so happens on Palm Sunday I am going thru the files and type out two pages of bits and pieces of old letters texts and what not and cut short bursts of this on the tape which I subsequently transferred to the typewriter and this page indicating where cut ins occur by the ///.

PALM SUNDAY TAPE

All he wants is out and I handed him the idea that if he cooperates with me he ought to make it ... & 'When You Walk Through A Storm' ... eager to please—You don't remember me? ... street voices ... throng of onlookers ... altar boy gone wrong ... echoes of the past ... old stolen car ... silver paper in the wind sun light on vacant lots ... that picture's awful dusty...Outside rain has fallen on the parched city...Please don't forget this small sad tale...dripping footsteps a seedy sky.

'Come in uh.' He looked at the slip 'uh Smith.' Wouldn't you except on Sundays? Does the past seep through? Dear Michael, how are your travel plans? Yeah well later on Oak St. That picture's awful dusty. Are you a member of the Union? Film Union 4 P.M.? Pink haired girl in Italy? Drums under the colonnade? *Je pense souvent en vous.* The soldier just said 'yes sir. Yes I believe in fate.'

'What are you up to?'

'Fish some...hunt...'

Not much time left on set sad menaces like pier ghosts goodbye two or three swans late on water.

'Come on now what? Why you waste time? Remember on Tuesday I opened his dresser drawer to find a bar of soap? Washed faces sunlight on the mirror the image in the mirror? Ever come back?

'I say what? What do you hunt for, George? You want to leave? hopeless stained with his birthplace...me alone...tired...fatigue...'

The kind of Martin Bradly he looked was an empty space-...there was nobody there—(Crew of 3 dead San Bruno California, Dec 24)—Clothes in sunlight...a crystal knee...afternoon against a misty Alpine Backdrop...cold sunlight seeps through the window and plays on the mirror the tall baroque mirror/ Street flesh diseased...outside the parched city...Dirty pictures shine? 'Little walk with me, Meester?'

"Drink this."

You are reading the future on formulae 5 channel 6 to record in writing our worn out film dim jerky far away.

"I say—"

Let's say you were phantom adolescent in 1920 roads—Douglas—Shadows on the closing film union blue are lights flickering empty streets sharp smell of weeds from old westerns.

'Behind you once Mister the violent evening sky. Sweet dreams Bradly, I am dying from a room in Princess Square.'

Cool remote spirit to his world of shades...this way to the

river on North Clark St. trying to get at my shoulder holster—
(They dyed my shoes)—still breathing persisting in mutilated
life—3 bullet holes fringed with jagged skin—they said they
were sorry about the news but his father was dead Old Arch
standing there with the cold spring news kerosene light blur-
ring his face out of focus dead fingers in smoke pointing to
Gibraltar. Weeping for lost cowbells and the odor of horse.

'Smell the horse? What do you see? Abandoned film . . . dying
hope . . . Don't ask questions for once. Hurry there isn't much
time. Adios from this address. Okay I am all through can't do
another thing.' Uncle Jim just kept saying: 'Son, all we did was
the best we could. We are the night family.' An open wound-
. . . money smeared with the blood of old movies.

'We hope to last? *Si me quieras* diseased bent over?'

Called in the sunlight Peter played with some rocks . . . a
single injection of radio active 'Old Days' . . . whisper of dark
streets in faded Panama photo weeping for the lost morning
there was nothing he could do about it that was the worst. Then
one day they called him to see this doctor and this is where I
began this story.

'Phil said I could begin it anyplace/'

Wonder what's left of old dream? sad muttering streets soiled
idiot body of scar tissue smelling of warm pyjamas at dawn.

'Hurry up please it is war everywhere. Just get those dirty
Panama pictures out of here blackout falling from the fountain.
Please help me up. Henry, Max, come over here. I want to pay.
Phil explosion in the dream mine. Know their mine?'

Plaintive call through remote dawn of backyards and ash
pits, 'I've come a long way with my pictures of a squirrel hunt.'

April 3, 1882. St. J. Missouri. A.M. Temperature 44—The sun
rose at 6:10—Wind was from the south east—It was a Monday—curtains of awakened rooms scrambled beds death whispering forgotten name.

'Yes, that's me there in the room waiting. Yes that's me
drifting after rotting pieces of himself on a picture dirtier than
my old house. That picture's awful dusty . . . (Yourself? *Quien
es?)*

Yes he was captured. Myself? *(Quien es?)* What do you see?

Abandoned film snaps in the wind. Every word cuts dying hope.'

'Ask him ... so ask him. Have guards present. That is an order.'

Dr. Albert Williams

'Bonjour—oui oui—Where are you? Your consul never paid a bill out of court.'

'Can I tell? I know let me tell.'

No repeat performance ... falls from a black Cadillac in 1920 roads ... music without passport ... Shonte Wetter—Mack the Knife —

You're still there 872 Golden Gate?' Silence by 1920 ponds in vacant lots. 'Take what is behind you once Mr. Bradly I am dying from a room in Quayquil—streets of fever and death. The consul glanced down at the slip on his desk 'And what can I do for you?' Hill St. poem R12 on my desk. Look at the time. We've waited a long time. Old answer back further and further—long ago morning—dead squirrel on a stump ... Glanced down at the slip on his desk 'When did you start drinking blood?' 'We find you lower.' Cool remote spirit drifted away into the woods. Know me in these foreign shit birds? Giver of winds is my name.'

Death is there waiting there long ago held a photograph in his withered hand.

'Know me in these foreign shit birds? Giver of Winds is my name'

Cool remote spirit to his world of shades.

ORE FROM DREAM MINE USED TO MAKE PALM SUNDAY TAPE

Why you waste time? I do not want to say that. Send someone. The police ball. For example you want to leave me alone. Tired. Fatigue. The street—little walk with me? The end—almost—if you like. 'Let's just say you were not ready. Phantom adolescent in violet evening sky. Sweet dreams sweet prince. Gordo dreams at at 117, 546 MPH Death's door—This way to the river—trying to get at my shoulder holster—papers in the air—think.'

59

Morning by a calm lagoon . . . in the bathroom at Price Road I float up to the ceiling and out the window / In the bedroom a black figure standing in the room with back turned to me. I remove the Russian hat he is wearing and we embrace. Sky whistles to a distant window, Mister I have opened naked a long time ago I folded the other childhood. Are you a member of the Union? Film Union 4 P.M. ???? The body of Mark Hayes is at the Sadlack Funeral Home. *Nueva Amenaza Para El Mundo:* La Sod. The Salvation May Come Precisely From The Sahara. In Sevilla an American subject kills himself throwing himself from a fourth floor. *(Cifra Thomas C. Shannon de 23 anos.)* We await a good chance. *Attendons une bonne chance.* Mr. Shannon no 'cept pay. Well that's about the closest way I know to tell you papers in an old scrapbook. Survey weeds cover this old hand. Don't remember me? Dim flickering silver of old dreams sad mutterings street boy voices on white steps of the sea wall. Outside rain has fallen on the parched city. Sahara Sahara we will soon be dry like you. Dear Michael how are your travel plans? Well yeah later at Oak St. *Je pense souvent en vous.* Sorry to be a year late in answering your letter. (sad menaces like pier ghosts are making him adieu). Unkinged goes the festival Dear Marc buy experience of me cheap psychoanalysis is a fraud. Cruel and hopeless stained with his birthplace flesh diseased dirty pictures. 'Shine Mister?' . . . No repeat performances. (Falls from a black Cadillac in 1920 roads). Take what is behind you once Meester Bradly. I am dying from a room in Quayquil—streets of fever and death—Old answer back further and further on North Clark Street—long ago morning with dead squirrel on a stump— What do you see? Abandoned film snaps in the afternoon wind ... every word cuts dying hope—this burning metal sickness—limestone ramps stained with excrement—'God damn it nurse I warned you about the Grey Ghost. Enemy of the 'people' Apo-Morphine in the dormitory.'

Why you waste time? I do not want experience to say that. For example you want to leave? hopeless stained with his birthplace—me alone—tired—fatigue—the street flesh diseased—dirty pictures shine?—little walk with me Mister?— Let's just say you were phantom adolescent in 1920 roads

Behind you once mister. The violet evening sky—sweet dreams Bradly—I am dying from a room in Princess Square. Streets of fever and death—this way to the river—on North Clark St. trying to get at my shoulder holster . . . what do you see? Abandoned film—dying hope—Don't ask questions for once hurry there isn't much time adios from this address. We hope to last? *Si me quieres* diseased bent over? a single injection of *radioactive* Old Days—Whisper of dark street in faded Panama photo—wonder what's left? of old dream sad muttering street? A soiled idiot body of cold scar tissue—plaintive calls through remote dawn of backyards and ash pits 'I've come a long way with my pictures of a squirrel hunt.'

Death whispering forgotten name—

'Yes that's me there in the room waiting. Yes that's me there drifting after rotting pieces of himself on a picture dirtier than my old house waiting there long ago the old picture torn across—(held a photograph in his withered hand)—feeling for a distant gun half buried in sand—far away back when 'Know me in these foreign shit bird? Giver of winds is my name.'

'Summer gold Course calling "Rain"/Pinned down under 1920 Spanish/Can't see my hand/!"

'Rain' bring glad tidings to 'Summer Gold Course'/'Cuff Links' washing 'Woolworths' down 'Cobble Stone Cody Can't get through with all the guards around/'

'Meet me in the florist shop/Come in on florist shop smell/'

Transient Rooms—wait for me a little longer—*por favor* $100—A man with raincoat drew darkness over the Socco Grande . . . 'do with a bit of dropsy—I know you've had it off—gold buying lark—It's the Fatima—Don't give the old beast a cent.' Time dilation—set your watches back an hour. Captain Clark welcomes you aboard lazy time tape of his home town. Few holes of golf? This languid paradise of dreamy skies and firefly evenings music across the golf course echoes from high cool corners of the dining room a little breeze stirs candles on the table. It was April afternoon. After a while some newsboy told him the war was over sadness in his eyes the trees filtering light on dappled grass the lake like bits of silver paper in a wind across the golf course—this story of a young man who lived as you and I do fading streets a distant sky. Body sadness to say 'goodbye.'

THE BEGINNING IS ALSO THE END

"I am not *an* addict. I am *the* addict. The addict I invented to keep this show on the junk road. I *am* all the addicts and all the junk in the world. I *am* junk and I am hooked forever. Now I am using junk as a basic illustration. Extend it. I am reality and I am hooked, on, reality. Give me an old wall and a garbage can and I can by God sit there forever. Because I am the wall and I am the garbage can. But I need some one to sit there and look at the wall and the garbage can. That is, I need a human host. I can't look at anything. I am blind. I can't sit anywhere. I have nothing sit on. And let me take this oportunity of replying to my creeping opponents. It is not true that I hate the human species. I just don't like human beings. I don't like animals. What I feel is not hate. In your verbal garbage the closest word is distaste. Still I must live in and on human bodies. An intolerable situation you will agree. To make that situation clearer suppose you were stranded on a planet populated by insects. You are blind. You are a drug addict. But you find a way to make the insects bring you junk. Even after thousands of years living there you still feel that basic structural distaste for your insect servants. You feel it every time they touch you. Well that is exactly the way I feel about my human servants. Consquently since my arrival some five hundred thousand years ago I have had one thought in mind. What you call the history of mankind is the history of my escape plan. I don't want 'love.' I don't want forgiveness. All I want is out of here."

Question: "Mr. Martin, how did all this start? How did you get here in the first place? If you found conditions so distasteful why didn't you leave at once?"

"Good questions I mean good questions, young man. Obviously I am not omnipotent. My arrival here was a wreck. The ship came apart like a rotten undervest. The accident in which I lost my sight. I was the only survivor. The other members of the crew ... well ... you understand ... uh sooner or later ... So I decided to act sooner. And I have acted sooner ever since. The entire human film was prerecorded. I will explain briefly how this is done. Take a simple virus illness like hepatitis. This illness has an incubation period of two weeks. So if I know when the virus is in (and I do because I put it there) I know how you will look two weeks from now: yellow. To put it another way: I take a picture or rather a series of pictures of you with hepatitis. Now I put my virus negatives into your liver to develop. Not far to reach: remember I live in your body. The whole hepatitis film is prerecorded two weeks before the opening scene when you notice your eyes are a little yellower than usual. Now this is a simple operation. Not all of my negatives develop by any means. All right now back to basic junk. Some character takes a bang of heroin for the first time. It takes maybe sixty consecutive shots before I can welcome another addict. (Room for one more inside, sir). Having taken one shot it becomes mathematically probable that taken, he will take another given the opportunity and I can always arrange that. Having taken two shots it becomes more probable that he will take a third. One negative developed makes others almost unavoidable. The same procedure can be applied to any human activity. If a man makes a certain amount of money by certain means he will go on making more money by the same means and so forth. Human activities are drearily predictable. It should now be obvious that what you call 'reality' is a function of these precisely predictable because prerecorded human activities. Now what could louse up a prerecorded biologic film? Obviously random factors. That is some one cutting my word and image lines at random. In short the cut up method of Brion Gysin which derives from Hassan I Sabbah and the planet Saturn. Well I've had a spot of trouble before but nothing serious. There was Rimbaud. And a lot of people you never heard of for good reasons. People who got too close one way or another. There was Tristan Tzara and the Surrealist Lark. I soon threw a block into that. Broke them all down to window dressers. So why didn't I stop Mr. Gysin in his tracks? I have ways of dealing with wise guys or I wouldn't be here. Early answer to use on anyone considering to interfere. Tricks I learned after the crash. Well perhaps I didn't take it seriously at first. And maybe I wanted to hear what he had to say about getting out. Always keep as many alternative moves open as possible. Next thing the blockade on planet earth is broken. Explorers moving in whole armies. And the usual do good missions talk about educating the natives for self government. And some hick sheriff from the nova heat charging me with 'outrageous colonial mismanagement and attempted nova.' Well they can't hang a nova rap on me. What I planned was simply to move out the biologic film to planet Venus and start over. Take along a few *good* natives to stock the new pitch and for the rest total disposal. That's not nova that's manslaughter. Second degree. And I planned it painless. I dislike screaming. Disturbs my medications. "

Question: "Mr. Martin, in the face of the evidence, no one can deny that nova was planned. The reports reek of nova."

"It will be obvious that I myself as an addict can only be a determined factor in some one else's equation. It's the old army game. Now you see me now you don't."

Question: "Mr. Martin, you say 'give me a wall and a garbage can and I can sit there forever.' Almost in the next sentence you say 'All I want is out of here.' Aren't you contradicting yourself?"

"You are confused about the word 'self.' I could by God sit there forever if I had a self to sit in that would sit still for it. I don't. As soon as I move in on any self all that self wants is to be somewhere else. Anywhere else. Now there you sit in your so called 'self.' Suppose you could walk out of that self. Some people can incidentally. I don't encourage this but it happens and threatens to become pandemic. So you walk out of your body and stand across the room. Now what form would the being that walks out of your body have? Obviously it would have precisely your form. So all you have done is take the same form from one place to another. You have taken great trouble and pain (believe me there is no pain like flesh withdrawal consciously experienced) and you have gotten precisely back where you started. To really leave human form you would have to leave human form that is leave the whole concept of word and image. You cannot leave the human image in the human image. You cannot leave human form in human form. And you cannot think or conceive in non-image terms by mathematical definition of a being in my biologic film which is a series of images. Does that answer your question? I thought not."

Question: "Mr. Martin, tell us something about yourself. Do you have any vices other than junk? Any hobbies? Any diversions?"

"Your vices other than junk I manipulate but do not share. Sex is profoundly distasteful to a being of my uh mineral origins. Hobbies? Chess. Diversions? I enjoy a good show and a good performer. Just an old showman. Well when you have to kill your audience every few years to keep them in their seats it's about time to pack it in."

Question: "Mr. Martin, I gather that your plan to move the show to planet Venus has, uh, miscarried. Is that correct?"

"Yeah it looks that way. The entire film is clogged."

Question: "In that case, Mr Martin where will you go when you go if you go?"

"That's quite a problem. You see I'm on the undesirable list with every immigration department in the galaxy. 'Who *him?* Don't let him out here.'"

Question: "Mr. Martin, don't you have any friends?"

"There are no friends. I found that out after the crash. I found that out before the others. That's why I'm still here. There are no friends. There are allies. There are accomplices. No one wants friends unless he is shit scared or unless he is planning a caper he can't pull off by himself."

Question: "Mr. Martin, what about the others who were involved in this crash? Aren't they still alive somewhere in some form?"

"You don't have to look far. They are sitting right here."

Question: "Who were these others?"

"There was an army colonel, a technician and a woman."

Question: "Won't you have to come to some sort of terms with your, uh, former accomplices?"

"To my disgruntled former associates I have this to say. You were all set to cross me up for the countdown. You think I can't read your stupid virus mind lady? And you, you technical bastard with your mind full of formulae I can't read. And you Colonel Bradley waiting to shoot me in the back. The lot of you. Blind and paralyzed I still beat you to the draw."

Question: "Mr. Martin, what sort of place did you people come from?"

"What sort of place did we come from. Well if you want the answer to that question, just look around, buster. Just look around."

"Ladies and Gentlemen, you have just heard an interview with Mr. Martin, sole survivor of the first attempt to send up a space capsule from planet earth. Mr. Martin has been called The Man Of A Thousand Lies. Well, he didn't have time for a thousand but I think he did pretty well in the time allotted. And I feel reasonably sure that if the other crew members could be here with us tonight they would also do a pretty good job of lying. But please remember that nothing is true in space. That there is no time in space—that what goes up under such auspices must come down—that the beginning is also the end.

"Ladies and gentlemen, these our actors bid you a long last good night."

From THE COLDSPRING NEWS

Coming through the pass a cold wind dried the sweat under his flannel shirt. The trail led down between black boulders into a green valley surrounded by the mountains on all sides. A stream ran through the valley, a network of streams in fact, the valley was crisscrossed with streams and pools of black deep water overhung by green turf. Painted with white paint on a black rock ten feet high, BLUE JUNCTION 2 MILES, an arrow pointing.

Late afternoon shadows on the water, fish jumping. The trail led through a grove of aspens and he could see the town ahead against the wall of blue mountains, like a toy town there in the distance.

A twilight like heavy blue dust was falling from the mountains when Martin rode into Blue Junction. He tied his horse to a hitching rail in front of the Last Cigarette Saloon and pushed open the swinging doors.

He did not feel talk stop as he entered. He felt that the men in the bar had been sitting standing without saying anything for some time before he walked in. That they had no need to talk and seldom did so.

Three men at the bar turned and looked at him. Then they looked beyond him at the door framed in blue light.

The bartender came slowly towards him as if from a great distance and leaned on the bar a heavy crippled question.

"Whisky. Sour mash whisky."

The bartender did not speak, he did not nod. He placed a bottle and glass on the bar.

Martin filled the glass. The silence fell heavy and blue. Martin could feel the silence inside. Occasional click of a glass on the polished oak bar, cards shuffled in a corner. He noticed that the players rarely spoke, indicating a raise by the number of chips shoved to the center of the table, a call by laying down their cards. Outside, frogs croaking from the valley.

Martin turned to the bartender.

"Do you have a room for tonight?"

The bartender nodded. He laid a heavy brass key on the bar. "Room 18, on the top floor. Livery stable across the street." Martin finished his drink and picked up the key.

ON THE BACK PORCH OF HIS FARM

Martin, Bradly Martin, Mr. Bradly Mr. Martin sat down on the back porch of his farm. He slipped a bag of Bull Durham out of is shirt pocket with two fingers and started rolling a cigarette. He paused listening. He finished rolling the cigarette, put it inside his lips and went back inside, lifted his gunbelt off a peg and hung it on. He lit the cigarette and sat down on the steps waiting.

Five horsemen stopped just outside the gate. They sat there looking at him and not saying anything.

Martin walked slowly out and leaned on the gate post. "Hello, Arch," he said addressing the oldest man. "Something on your mind?"

"Well, yes Martin, you might say so. Thought maybe some of my stock might have strayed up here?"

"Not that I know of, Arch, but this is free range country fellers say."

"Maybe a little too free, Martin."

"Don't know as I understand you, Arch." His grey eyes pinned out in the afternoon sun cold as metal glinting to a distant point.

"Just telling you Martin I been losing a lot of stock lately."

"Why tell me, Arch?" said Martin softly.

"Because Clem here seen you the other day in Cold Spring selling off some stock."

"So?"

"Looked to me like the brand had been changed," said Clem keeping his eyes on the pummel of his saddle. Martin shifted his around Clem at the pale blue summer sky: "How close were you, Clem?"

"Just about as close as I am to you now."

"That's mighty close, Clem. Funny I didn't see you."

"You had your back turned."

"Well it isn't turned now, Clem."

Martin just stood there after that not saying anything and there wasn't anything to say—just cigarette smoke drifting in the still afternoon and Martin's pinpoint metal eyes looking through the smoke. Arch turned his horse abruptly. The party rode away. Martin went back and sat down on the porch steps.

WAITING THE SURVEY LINE QUITE SOME YEARS

Martin sat down on the golf course kinda run down now rolling a cigarette that building was torn down walked back inside gun right on the survey line. They sat there.

"Look folks don't own what they thought."

Martin walked slowly out to 'The Big Survey' and leaned on the gate post quite some years ... "Surveying your mind nice and cozy thought maybe some of my June time might have strayed up here—free range country—afternoon wind—??"

"Back to the spring house. Understand you. Arch."

This is the way the world I created whispers between years saddest of all movies caught and say so. Gun looking right through the other field of vision won't cross no more bridges. Sad voices dirtier older pretend it's someone else at recess time waiting a shredded belt blurred yellow ribs distant 1920 wind and dust: "I have opened the gates for you." He waves his hand sadly from the lake from the hill from the sky. Remember the boy's room is quite empty now books and toys put away soldier's goodbye on a windy street half buried in sand. Dead stars splash his cheek bone with silver ash. Klinker is dead. The Piper pulled down the sky. Caught in New York beneath the animals of the village the Piper pulled down the sky. Now he didn't go alooking for to show you the papers clear as 'Annie Laurie' in any naborhood bar just telling you. Martin, see this price?"

"Why tell me, Arch?" said the dead leaves and there was a blue shirt and cigarette smoke drifting near future air against the pale gun. 'I didn't see you' marks the spot: Martin's British ultimatum of peace or war.

Fresh southerly winds a long time ago over New York shirt flapping with the torn sky a distant hand lifted. "Good bye, Mister. Used to be the man you're looking for. Couldn't reach. Breath never called opportunity to do so." 'September 17, 1899, cool remote Sunday' last resort. Come closer. Listen. Station ends the last smell of blood and excrement whispered on a fence, 'Goodbye, Mister.'

SAD SERVANT OF THE INLAND SIDE

Silent grocer shops cobblestone streets and the lake like bits of silver paper in the wind hard across the gold course. Sad servant of the inland side offered us his pictures of a squirrel hunt where the second hand book shop used to be right opposite the old cemetery and you couldn't find a pleasanter place to sit on your June time last gun post erased in a small town newspaper making the stars run backward again when the old man died like the train did.

"How many times I tell him" it's far away for the last time dead folks talk erased out against the frayed stars from his gun a rusty answer drew September 17, 1899.

Over New York a flaming hand across the sky dim jerky far away some one had shut a bureau drawer. A distant soldier never came out at recess time that afternoon I watched the torn sky bend with the wind white white white as the eye can see a blinding flash of white the cabin reeks of exploded star. It was a long time ago young man can still see used to be your brother young cop whistling 'Annie Laurie' if my memory serves on the top, on the top floor though I wouldn't advise . . . state it's in . . . kinda run down now you can still see the old fence there by creek water washing around his bare feet silver ghost boy of exploded star.

He dropped the photo into a bureau drawer smell of ashes rising from the typewriter a black silver sky of broken film. Wasn't anything to say. 'Mr. Bradly Mr. Martin stood there on dead stars heavy with his dusty answer drew 'September 17, 1899' over New York he waves his hands sadly turns them out:

"Giving you my toy soldiers" put away steps trailing down a windy street exploded star between us.

Sad muttering street boy voices on white steps of the sea wall. 'You come with me, Meester?' J's words once. Yes all the words were mine once. With a telescope you can watch our worn out film dim jerky far away shut a bureau drawer."

WHO IS THE

THIS is a story
in *three* columns
moving at differ
ent speeds (he
holds up *three*
flickering silver
fingers) in this
column we have
every-day life
plain decent bone
mean men and wom
en going about
their dirty rotten
jobs Rock Ape
Waiter there with
the wrong wine
ugly American
snarl this a
story of a short
trip 24 frames
just like it hap
pened to me when
I say a cop with
walkie-talkie I
mean just that in
present time
trip from Tangier
to Gibraltar
Algeciras Ceuta
Tetuon and re-
turn to Tangier

'Where did he
die?'
'On my breath in
the Saloon of
The Mons
Calpe cold coff
ee sitting right
where you are
sitting now
Travel Date 10/
4/64 Ticket 23

WALKS BESIDE YOU

In this column of var
ying speed and distan
I digress to drop a
(parenthesis of years)
Tangier Gibraltar
Gibraltar Tangier I
can't read this card it
it's all in Arabic
'Captain Clark welcom
es you aboard set your
watches forward or
back an hour depend-
ing which way you come
on it In
April I was looking
through some material
graciously placed at
my disposal by Rives
Mathews old friend and
neighbor (pronounc
ed *Reeves* from 4660
Berlin Avenue changed
it to Pershing in the
war St Louis Mo The
Veiled Prophet
Ball memories of St
Louis letters of a
young editor with re
ference to Mr T.S.
Eliot beside you with
a coffee tray of
visiting cards under
glass many of them
inscribed with mess-
ages I cannot resist
a quotation 'Comte
Wladimir Sollohub
Rashid Ali Khan Bre
mond d'Ars Marquis
de Migre Principe
di Castelcicale
Gentilhoma di Pal-
azzo your a long

WRITTEN 3RD?

16 frames per sec
ond old film here
dim jerky far
away you can see
Bradly Martin gun
jumping in his
hand sharp smell
of weeds from old
Westerns reading
intersections dur-
ing the trip I
was reading *The
Wonderful Country*
by Mr Tom Lea
Special Student
Edition is the
story of Martin
Bradly of Missouri
who took refuge
in Mexico from a
murder charge and
there worked as
a pistolero carry
ing a gun for the
Castro brothers I
started reading
*The Wonderful
Country* in the
Panama Restaurant
So returning various
bits and pieces of
the picture from the
White Reader I read:
'The Blue Indians
of North Carolina
greet you from a
West that is dying
that's about the
closest way I know
to tell you *And
papers rustling
across the city
desks* ... fresh south-

I left Tangier Tuesday St. June 23, 1964 and returned Friday 26 before I re late the events that took place in a short trip home I will mention a cur ious *incident* that took place a few days prior to June 23. I had stepped quietly into the street from 16 rue Delacroix Tangier quiet ly you understand so as not to stir the gu ides and ambulant vendors who abound in these waters. (Just at that moment the bus for the *Hotel Pasadena* drove past). It would seem that I had not stepped quietly enough. A newspaper vendor approached me. 'English paper, Mister? Daily Telegraph?' I handed him 60 moroc can francs. The price of the paper is 58 fr. He said, 'Six pesetas *Spanish* money. This Moroccan money' and handed it back. 'So' I said 'This is also Morocco. Not Spain.' He took the paper ba ck saying 'That is *yesterday's* paper' He walked away with a closed expression. No-

way from St Louis' At this point an announcement came over the radio: 'Now pay attention we are going to g- ive a few hints... *You will win a roo m in a first class hotel for two peop- le*... Ticket to *Se- ville* and return... April Fair in *Se- ville*'... I incor- porated this radio message into the text... Into the sp- eaking clock... the speaking clock tel ling you his past history. Let me tell you about a score of years dust on the window one sum mer the speaking clock his past hi- story a long time ago fresh southerly winds from remote landing that after noon I watched the torn sky bend with the wind return v- arious bits and pieces of the picture dim flick- ering on the tele from *Spain.* Yes, boys, that's me th- ere, 'Sad Poison Nice Guy.' You know I'm selling *Spain Repeat Performance Page. Boy of Decay ing Dream.* So your looking from the B- elleview Hotela are

erly winds a long time ago... page 13 Student Edition... *Good adjutants out there in the wind* Remember *Tuesday St Benjamin's Day This is the end of* Mars *March* Marzo Whole sky burning agony to breathe *here*... page 15... *Un ited States Mail Route 39094* Flight *No 61066* Tangier Gibraltar... Set your clocks foreward an hour... Set watches forward an hour... page 25... *as if it came from a long way off and hadn't found anything*... sad shrinking face... he had come a long way for something not exchanges... he died during the ni- ght... page 43... *The kind of Martin Bradly he looked for was an empty place. There was nobody there*... used to be the man you were looking for used to be the man steps trailing a lonely dining room sad train whistles in a distant sky... page 52 outside *around the crumbled* towers the wind made a sighing sound back back to page 25 *as if it came from a long way off and* w understand that these ambulant vendors of newspapers are such dedicated short changers as to be mortally offended when one gives the correct change and no chance to paw through the coins in one's hand. None the less they do not refuse a sale. Clearly something *special* had been said *That is yesterday's paper... Spanish money.* Something to remember the words and the closed expression. Son on June 23, Tuesday, St Jacob I was waiting in the *Panama* restaurant on Boulevard Pasteur for the bus to the airport. I was reading *The Wonderful Country* hurry and wait. They told me in *Cook's* the bus would be in front of *American Express* at *2:10 pm*. The bus did not arrive until *3 o'clock in the afternoon.* Set your clocks forward an hour. The flight will last approximately 20 minutes. We will be flying at a height of 2,000 feet. Arriving approximately 20 minutes later in Gibraltar. 'And where will you be staying in Gibraltar, Mr Burroughs?'... thin grey official tired

you young man? used to be the Pass Hotel if my memory serves... well when you come to the *Old Signal Tower*... though I wouldn't advise climbing it state it's in... so sight ing from the *East Beach*... 130 youths on the beach... you can't exactly see the hotel but you can see where it is if the wind is right and that's about the closest way I know to tell you unless you want to see Arch's maps... Don't rightly think

'Captain Clark welcomes you aboard.'

Arch himself could make them out ... Last rites for 44 airliner dead including Captain *Clark* (left)... left an old junkie selling Christmas seals on North *Clark* St. The Priest they called him. Just an old friend left between worlds... your middle

hadn't found anything On page 89 is a picture hand with a cocked revolver... *The barber's scissors clicked at the back of Martin's head* on page 90 *'It is permissible to shoot and kill one who tries to escape the custody of his employer without his employer's consent and without having paid all his debts in full....* Takes me back to page 71 ... Letter there to **Martin Bradly:** *You will remain in the charge of* Senor Sterner *until you are fit for my service when you will receive instructions for further employment during your idleness at the border* (on page 85 I crossed the Spanish frontier) *you will make yourself useful listening for such information as may be of interest to me. I remain Your Attentive and Faithful Servant Cipriano Castro* This letter is in the estilo of my Paris publisher who resembles Cipriano Castro in appearance and manner. So what are waiters but pistoleros? hired killers?

grey priest voice. 'Hotel Victoria' I sa id without convict ion. He wondered peev ishly if he might not find every hotel in Gib staffed with dim distant Rock Apes... 'A *single* room sir? We have no rooms at all.' I walked out a door at the end of the airport... no taxi... turned a corner of the building and loo ked into the calm eyes of a Spanish adolescent who had just urinated against the wall... taxi... 'Hotel Vic- toria'... A cop with a walkie-talkie directed us back to the first cop... no road through... I start ed to walk... cop stopp ed me. 'Sorry sir you can't go through... Changing of the guard you know' arriving at the Hotel Victoria by a circuitous route I was not surprised to find that the Hotel Victoria was full. So I took a cab and did what I should have done at the fir st check point: dir- ected him to take me to the new hotel on the *East Beach.* 'Do you have a single room?' 'No sir but we have a *double* room'

aged reporter Mr Cost...

Please remember I have no hope no hope at all... De lito mayor del homb re es haber nacido the sky pilots tell us... sad voices dirtier older... 'Are th- er any cigarettes? Will you please ta- ke a cup of tea up to the workman on the roof?' These houses all leak. My old friend Rives Mathews had his roof fixed three times and it still leaks so pay attention we are going to give a few hints Now we have three columns here (He held up three flickering silver fingers sweat ing last human pieces *here*)... Column one com es under the heading of *news*... arrivals... departures. incidents... hotels... *(First class)*... dates *(April)*... places (like *Seville).* High Society... (Happy Comte Hector Perrone di San Martino, Mrs Edge at home last Thursday in May... Fete-Dieu Now what in Helen Sapiola de Cobo Quai d'Oroay Prince Paul Troubetsky Contessa di Hell does that mean?)... Column one

It has to be written before it happens

We write death... In the late summer of 1957 if my memory se rves I just happen- ed to be in Algiers Milk Bar there on main drag vats of passion fruit, whipped cream, colored syrups mirrors around the walls and square mir ror columns refract- ing a milk bar scene. Well now about a month or so later if my me mory serves (I was in Tangier at the time) bomb in the milk bar yielded 12 casualties So when I come to the milk bar in *The Quiet American* by Graham Greene look around and see it is the same milk bar and hit the deck... *twelve* year old boy there both legs blown off spattered with mara schino cherries, blood, brains and whipped cream... 'Was that a grenade?' he said... But then who am I to be critical... 44 airl- iner dead... The Priest there hand lifted... Can you hear me Capta in Greene and all you jokers in the Shakes- peare Squadron? Pls toleros, hired killers In 1957 I wrote... 'The soccer scores are com

First class all right
two beds...bath...tele
phone...The hotel was
surrounded by signal
towers...I took a bath
and lay down on the
bed which would be
on the right if you
were standing at the
head of the beds...
Outside the wind wh-
istled through the
towers and rattled the
white plastic blinds.
At 7 pm (set your
clocks forward an
hour) I dressed and
proceeded to the Am-
erican Bar...potted
plants along the wall
potted plants painted
on the wall...patches
of painted brick...
mural of a bull fight
poster: 'Plaza de Tor
os...Real Maestranza
de *Seville...Avril*
fiestas ... Carlos Cor
buchi...Antonio Ord
onez, Cesar Giron...'
Real mastery of *Sev-
ille...April*...The food
and service first cl
ass...After dinner I
retired to my room
read for an hour and
so to bed...
Breakfast—taxi...

is the *cloth*, toros,
to distract you from
intersection points
in column 2 and 3...
You are carrying out
a complex decoding
operation in a sub-
way rush hour. Now
column 2 consists of
miscellaneous inter-
section points with
column 1 and 3.
That is to say mem-
ories of past word and
image...No 3 consists
of intersections in
a text read at the
time with the news
and memory columns...
This is the *third*
lesson...Stop charging
the *news* column...Look
behind the news...Look
under the news for
intersection points
You travel on I.P.'s

ing in from the capit
al...One must pretend
an interest, ... *298
Known Dead In Lima
Soccer Riot* Tuesday
May 26, 1964...The soc
cer scores are still
coming in ... dead child
there crushed against
gates of the stadium.
Pistoleros, hired kill
ers who hires you to
write the formulae
of disasters, wars,
riots and death for
the *News*...Who hires
you to write *The Cold
Spring News?* Publisher
s. They have had enou
gh out of our hides. It
is time to do our own
publishing. All right
tv Tome your turn now

The driver told me
that the highest tow
er. (Well over 200 ft.
and projecting above
the Rock) is known as
The Old Signal Tower

Police of Chief in Baghdad for Chrisakes .. The grey guards .. *Guarda
su pistola listo hombre* .. The treasury calls it illegal tender ..
The barn boy there .. Test trio share a horse across his *cojones*

The porter at the door for the rent .. Now here is the glyph for
house .. Just a square with an opening .. Through that opening you
can see a house at No 16 Bournemouth Road, London .. And here i Ian

And here is Jennifer's Diary .. Pied Piper Ball .. dark room .. old huma
human voices .. Let me quietly Fliday .. This was Hector Perrone di
Delicious Diner Gracious Newman San Martin .. Nicky Embirico and

Mrs Fiona Musker hearted third .. Have you forgotten late in human
voices .. And here is the glyph for 'white house' treasury .. Hummm
looks like a poppy pod growing through the house .. 'Past the Ameri

can he could plainly see grey junk yesterdays trailing the earth
Fete dieu last Thursday in May .. And now Danny Pre Door notations
from the broken maps .. sundry nations decaying on the city desk ..

Washed back on Spain Repeat Performance page farm boy in the barn
sad poison Fabian socialist .. everybody does it here .. 'I'm glad
you are *here,'* Mr. Wilson' .. *sa-di ma-li—dama lai maquaih* writing

what Tuesday shanta shanta .. T. (for Terrence) Heming .. Remember me
Mrs Murphy .. Old junkie left on North Clark St .. May amigo in Spain
understood now .. That God damned Board hit me .. There I was bound

hand and foot .. young street flesh .. rubbing sticky .. his warm hands
caressed my body .. *tres peu de temps?* William .. In desperate battle
Old Arch there with the Cold Spring News you come to where I fin

ished carrying a .22 rifle dim jerky far away offered us his
pictures of a squirrel hunt—silent grocer shops .. cobblestone
streets the lake like bits of silver paper in a wind hard across

the golf course .. Old human voices erased out against the frayed
stars .. A flaming hand drew September 17, 1899 over New York ..
Last gun post erased in a small town newspaper making the stars

run backwards again like the train did .. Dim jerky far away some
one had shut a bureau drawer .. His rusty gun for the last time
smoke against the dead stars .. And that's about the closest way I

know to tell you and papers rustling across the city desk . . All
the news that's fit to print fresh southerly winds a long time
ago . . Special to The New York Times September 17, 1899 . . Seth Low

On Rampago Job . . The Treasurey Calls It Illegal Tender . .
Jewel Tea Company Inc. Pay to the BEARER five cents . .
Barn boy there . . date Vietnam . . Ranch Co. To Or-

ganized . . *Exposicion de un Pintor Venezolano en el Casion
Municipal* . . The Grey Guards there . . Glasses rattling in Emsallah
Gardens . . Blast very close now . . The flag is down on Surete Nationale

Writing in the policeman? We own cops out of Hell now . . all the
Grey Guards . . Mr Martin waves from a sepia park . . Street crowds in
Bagdad rising from the typewriter . . Mr. Bradly smiles. Dim jerky far

away stars splash his cheek bones with silver ash off the
electric ticker already negotiating Japanese tourist program intend
ed that British investments in the United States African 'Common

Market' plan among Kenya & Uganda's purchases from 'Tanzan' limit
Safeway Tanganyika exports under a quota system by H.M. Harper
Chinese rockets reading reliable gun shots off the electric ticker

ST. LOUIS RETURN

(ticket to St. Louis and return in a first class room for two people who is the third that walks beside you?) After a parenthesis of more than 40 years I met my old neighbor, Rives Skinker Mathews, in Tangier. I was born 4664 Berlin Avenue changed it to Pershing during the war. The Mathews family lived next door at 4660—red brick three-story houses separated by a gangway large back yard where I could generally see a rat one time or another from my bedroom window on the top floor. Well we get to talking St. Louis and "what happened to so and so" sets in and Rives Mathews really knows what happened to any so and so in St. Louis. His mother had been to dancing school with "Tommy Eliot"—(His socks wouldn't stay up. His hands were clammy. I will show you far in dancing school)— Allow me to open a parenthesis you see Rives Mathews had kept a scrapbook of St. Louis years and his mother left a collection of visiting cards from the capitals of Europe. I was on my way back to St. Louis as I looked through Rives' scrapbook dim flickering pieces of T. S. Eliot rising from the pages—(But what have I my friend to give you put aside on another tray? Those cards were burned in my winter house fire, October 27, 1961—Comte Wladmir Sollohub Rashis Ali Khan Bremond d'ars Marquis de Migre St. John's College 21 Quai Malaquais Principe de la Tour—Gentilhomo di Palazzo—you're a long way from St. Louis and vice versa.)

"I want to reserve a drawing-room for St. Louis."

"A drawing-room? Where have you been?"

"I have been abroad."

"I can give you a bedroom or a roomette as in smaller."

"I will take the bedroom."

6:40 P.M. Loyal Socks Rapids out of New York for St. Louis— Settled in my bedroom surrounded by the luggage of ten years abroad I wondered how small a roomette could be. A space capsule is where you find it. December 23, 1964, enlisting the aid of my porter, a discreet Oriental personage and a far cry indeed from old "Yassah Boss George" of my day, a table was installed in this bedroom where I could set up my Facit portable and type as I looked out the train window. Snapping an occasional picture with my Zeiss Ikon, I could not but lament the old brass spittoons, the smell of worn leather, stale cigar smoke, steam iron and soot. Looking out the train window—click click clack—back back back—Pennsylvania Railroad en route four people in a drawing room::::One leafs through an old joke magazine called *LIFE:*—("What we want know is who put the sand in the spinach?")—A thin boy in prep school clothes thinks this is funny. Ash gathers on his father's Havana held in a delicate gray cone the way it holds on a really expensive cigar. Father is reading *The Wall Street Journal.* Mother is putting on the old pancake, *The Green Hat* folded on her knee. Brother—"Bu" they call him—is looking out the train window. The time is 3 P.M. The train is one hour out of St. Louis, Missouri. Sad toy train it's a long way to go see on back each time place what I mean dim jerky far away. */Take/* Look out the window of the train. Look. Postulate an observer Mr. B from Pitman's Common Sense Arithmetic at Point X one light hour away from the train. Postulate further that Mr. B. is able to observe and photograph the family with a telescopic camera. Since the family image moving at the speed of light will take an hour to reach Mr. B., when he takes the 3 P.M. set the train is pulling into St. Louis Union Station at 4 P.M. St. Louis time George the porter there waiting for his tip. (Are you a member of the Union? Film Union 4 P.M.?) The family will be met at the station by plain Mr. Jones or Mr. J. if you prefer. (It was called Lost Flight. Newspapers from vacant lots in a back alley print shop lifted bodily out of a movie set the Editor Rives Mathews. Mr. and Mrs. Mortimer Burroughs and their two sons Mortimer Jr. and William Seward Burroughs of 4664 Berlin Avenue changed it to Pershing during the war. I digress I digress.)

Postulate another observer Mr. B-1 at Point X-1 two light hours away. The train in his picture is now two light hours out of St. Louis at 2 P.M. still in the dinner. The train is stopped by a vacant lot distant 1920 wind and dust */Take/* remote foreign suburbs—end of a subdivision street—What a spot to land with a crippled ship—sad train whistles cross a distant sky. See on back what I mean each time place dim jerky far away not present except in you watching a 1920 movie out the train window? Returning to 1964 or what's left of it—December 23, 1964, if my memory serves I was thinking about a friend in New York name of Mack Sheldon Thomas not a finer man in Interzone than old S.T. has this loft apartment and every time he leaves the bathroom door open there is a rat gets in the house so looking out the train window I see a sign: Able Pest Control /Take/

"I tell you boss when you think something you see it—all Mayan according to the Hindu philosophizers," observed B.J. who fortunately does not take up any space in the bedroom.

"B.J. there is no call to theorize from a single brass spittoon or even a multiple smell of worn leather. You know I dislike theories."

"George! the nudes!"—(He knew of course that the nudes would be waiting for me in front of the Union Station.)

Look out the train window/Take/:acres of rusting car bodies—streams crusted with yesterday's sewage—American flag over an empty field—Wilson Stomps Cars—City of Xenia Disposal—South Hill a vast rubbish heap—Where are the people? What in the name of Christ goes on here? Church of Christ /Take/ crooked crosses in winter stubble—The porter knocks discreetly.

"Half an hour out of St. Louis, sir."

Yes the nudes are still there across from the station recollect once returning after a festive evening in East St. Louis hit a parked car 60 MPH thrown out of the car rolled across the pavement and stood up feeling for broken bones right under those monumental bronze nudes by Carl Milles Swedish sculptor depict the meeting of the Missouri and Mississippi river waters. It was a long time ago and my companion of that remote evening is I believe dead. (I digress I digress).

But what has happened to Market Street the skid row of my adolescent years? Where are the tattoo parlors, novelty stores, hock shops—brass knucks in a dusty window—the seedy pitchmen—("This museum shows all kinds social disease and self abuse. Young boys need it special"—Two boys standing there can't make up their mind whether to go in or not—One said later "I wonder what was in that lousy museum?")—Where are

81

the old junkies hawking and spitting on street corners under the gas lights?—distant 1920 wind and dust—box apartments each with its own balcony—Amsterdam—Copenhagen—Frankfurt—London—anyplace.

Arriving at the Chase Plaza Hotel I was shown to a large double room a first class room in fact for two people. Like a good European I spent some time bouncing on the beds, testing the hot water taps, gawking at the towels the soap the free stationery the television set—(And they call *us* hicks).

"This place is a paradise," I told B.J.

And went down to the lobby for the local papers which I check through carefully for items or pictures that intersect amplify or illustrate any of my writings past present or future. Relevant material I cut out and paste in a scrapbook—(some creaking hints—*por eso* I have survived) Relevant material I cut out and paste in a scrapbook—(Hurry up please it's time)— For example, last winter I assembled a page entitled *Afternoon Ticker Tape* which appeared in *My Magazine* published by Jeff Nuttall of London. This page, an experiment in newspaper format, was largely a rearrangement of phrases from the front page of *The New York Times,* September 17, 1899, cast in the form of code messages. Since some readers objected that the meaning was obscure to them I was particularly concerned to find points of intersection, a decoding operation you might say relating the text to external coordinates: (From *Afternoon Ticker Tape:* "Most fruitful achievement of the Amsterdam Conference a drunk policeman"). And just here in the *St. Louis Globe Democrat* for December 23, I read that a policeman has been suspended for drinking on duty slobbed out drunk in his prowl car with an empty brandy bottle—(few more brandies neat)—(From *A.T.T.:* "Have fun in Omaha")—And this item from Vermillion, S.D.: "Omaha Kid sends jail annual note and $10"—Please use for nuts food or smokes for any prisoners stuck with Christmas in your lousy jail" signed "The Omaha Kid"—(From *A.T.T.:* "What sort of eels called Retreat 23?")— *St. Louis Globe Democrat:* "A sixth army spokesman stated two more bodies recovered from the Eel River. Deaths now total 23."—(From *A.T.T.:* "Come on Tom it's your turn now")—*St. Louis Post Dispatch:* "Tom Creek overflows its banks."

Unable to contain himself B.J. rolled on the bed in psycho-phantic convulsions: "I tell you boss you write it and it happens. Why if you didn't write me I wouldn't be here."

I told him tartly that such seeming coincidence was no doubt frequent enough if people would just keep their eyes and ears open. We descended to The Tenderloin Room for dinner where I was introduced to an American speciality: baked potato served with sour cream. Ausgezeichnet.

"I tell you boss you couldn't touch this food in Paris for anywhere near the price."

The next day very mild and warm I walked around the old neighborhood which is not far to walk now the old Bixby place used to be right where the hotel is now and I passed it every day as a child on my way to Forest Park with brother "Bu" and our English governess who always told me:—"Don't ask questions and don't pass remarks"—. This cryptic injunction I have been forced to disregard for professional reasons, you understand. So prowling about with my camera looking for 1920 scraps— bits of silver paper in the wind—sunlight on vacant lots—The Ambassador—"Home With A Heart"—where an old friend Clark St. lived—4664 still there looking just the same—("Do you mind if I take a few pictures? used to live here you know.")—so few people on the street—Convent Of The Sacred Heart—This message on a stone wall—"Gay—Lost—" the houses all look empty—It was not given to me to find a rat but I did photograph several squirrels (offered us his pictures of a squirrel hunt)—So back to my quiet remote room and my scrapbooks.

"Ash pits—an alley—a rat in the sunlight—It's all here," I tapped my camera," all the magic of past times like the song says right under your eyes back in your own back yard. Why are people bored? Because they can't see what is right under their eyes right in their own back yard. And why can't they see what is right under their eyes?—(Between the eye and the object falls the shadow)—And that shadow, B.J., is the *pre-re-corded word.*"

"Oh sir you slobbered a bimfull."

"Like I come out here to see 'a bunch of squares in Hicks-ville'? Well I will see just that. I come here to see what I see and

83

that's another story. Any number of stories. Walk around the block keeping your eyes open and you can write a novel about what you see—down in the lobby last night—smoky rose sunset across the river."

"The river is in the other direction boss."

"So what? Shift a few props. Now would you believe it people are sitting there with their back to that sunset."

"I don't want to believe it boss."

"B.J., remember the roller coaster at Forest Park Highlands.?"

"I sure do boss. Why one time me and that Mexican girl used to work in the Chink laundry on Olive Street—"

"All right, B.J. cut. From now on we run a clean show. A show you can take your kids and your grandmother to see it. Just good clean magic for all the family. Remember Thurston?"

"I sure do boss. He made a white elephant disappear."

"Exactly—a white elephant—all our gray junk yesterdays—everything sharp and clear like after the rain."

At this point B. J. jumped to his feet, opened an umbrella and bellowed out "April Showers"—(White rain sloshed down—a wall of water you understand.)

"All right, B.J., Cut!"

Sunday December 27 driving around St. Louis with brother "Bu" stopping here and there to take pictures—The Old Courthouse and all the records /Take/ and there by the river across the river depending on which way you come on it is the arch still under construction at that time 600 feet high when they finished it—(Gateway To The West)—has an ominous look like the only landmark to survive an atomic blast or other natural catastrophe /Take/ cobblestone streets along the levee—refuge of river boat days—strata of brick and masonry—geology of a city—MacArthur Bridge /Take/ and just *there* a truck will crash through the guard rail and fall 75 feet killing the driver you can see the dotted line in the *Post Dispatch* picture /Take/ River Queen and the Admiral just like they used to be red plush guilt the lot cruising down the river on a Sunday afternoon.

"Shall we take in the West End?"

Clayton and the West End suburbs now built up beyond

recognition after 20 years absence. In the 1920's my family moved out west on the Price Road—(700S. /*Take*/ and just down the road is the John Burroughs School and there is the locker room door /*Take*/ where I stood one afternoon a long time ago and watched the torn sky bend with the wind lightning struck the school just *there/Take/*(Whoever said lightning never strikes twice in the same place was no photographer.)—1929 tornado if my memory serves when all the records went up name and address old arch there by the river with the cold spring news.

"Cruising Down the River on a Sunday Afternon"—(This music across the water—The Veiled Prophet Ball off stage)—On the scene photographs by William Born Field *St. Louis Magazine* 52, Retarded Children's Project, young St. Louis citizens bicentennial salute: (Happy New Year Comte Hector Perrone de San Martine Mrs. Edge at home last Thursday in May, Fete Dieu, Principe de la Tour, Gentilhomo di Palazzo, you're a long retarded children project veiled way from St. Louis. I, Famous Bar Prophet, had not thought Death Magazine 52 had undone so many for I have known them all: Baron Rashid Pierre de Cobo—Helen Zapiola Theresa Riley—I digress ï digress.)

"Now what in Horton Vernet Gen-San Martine Zapiolo The Swan Last Day de Cobo Principe di Castel Hose it Chicale Randy Vieled Miguel Garcia de Rube Gordon Hell does that mean?" interjected B.J.

(A long review—human voices—*They* expected answers?)

Family Reunion at my Aunt K's. B.J. has observed with his usual astuteness in such matters that there is only half a bottle of whiskey on the side board, volunteered for bartender duty surreptitiously serving himself double measure so when another bottle is produced rather sooner than later we both feel a little well you know B.J. is an old Alcohol Anonymous as used to electrify the meetings with his confessions: "Once at the house of a friend" he begins sepulchrally "in the dead of night—I"—he stabs a finger at his chest—"sneaked into the room of my host's adolescent son." He tiptoes across the platform and turns to the audience. "You get the picture?" The audience stirs uneasily. B.J. shifts an imaginary flashlight—

"arrowheads—a stone axe—butterfly trays—the cyanide jar—a stuffed owl—Whoo whoo whoo drank the alcohol off the boy's preserved centipede?"—It was emetic in the good sense. (I digress—a drunk policeman—Stein reverts to his magazine.)

I address myself to a cousin who is now account executive for an advertising firm: "What I say is time for the artist and the ad man to get in a symbiotic way and give birth to what we may call 'Creative Advertising' I mean advertisements that tell a story and create character. Like this see? So you handle the Southern Comfort account?"

"Ty Bradly river boat gambler at your service, suh." His blue eyes fixed quizzically on the barmaid's ample bosom, he drawled out "I'll take double Southern Comfort, Ma'am."

"Pardon me are you Colonel Bradly? Colonel Ty Bradly?"

Bradly turned to face the question his eyes unbluffed unreadable two fingers in a vest pocket rested lightly on the cold blue steel of his Remington derringer.

"I am suh."

"Yeah and think what we could do with the Simmons Mattress account," interjected B.J.

(All right, B.J., /Cut!/) See what I mean? glamour—romance—Inspector J. Lee of the Nova Police smokes Players—(flashes his dirty rotten hunka tin)—Agent K9 uses a Bradly laser gun—Advertisements should provide the same entertainment value as the content of a magazine. *Your* product deserves the best. Why make up silly jingles? Why not use the good old songs like "Annie Laurie." There's a story goes with that song. Remember a young cop whistling "Annie Laurie" down cobblestone streets? Then he stopped in the corner saloon for a glass of Budweiser which he couldn't have done really being on duty. Yes he would have approved your favorite smoke. Show your cards all *Players*. And remember a young cop whistling "Annie Laurie" down cobblestone streets twirling his club drew September 17, 1899 over St. Louis.

(The sky goes out against his back.)

Mr. Dickson Terry of the *St. Louis Post Dispatch* interviews your reporter: "As you know in the 1890's St. Louis was famous throughout the world for such restaurants as Tony Faust—But when I was last here 20 years ago there was not a first class eating place to be found in the city—You might say all the uh flavor had been siphoned off into the subdivisions and country clubs of the West End—This process is now being reversed— any number of excellent restaurants—three in fact right here in the Chase Plaza Hotel—a movement *back* to the city—*back* to the 1890's finds expression in Gas Light Square and the refurbished river boats—yes decidedly the reversal of a trend which I for one found deplorable—and that is what I am getting at in this seemingly obscure passage." I taped a text on the table between us, a text using the three column format of a small town newspaper.

THE MOVING TIMES
September 17, 1899 Mr Bradly
Mr Martin stood there on dead
stars heavy with his dusty
answer drew September 17,
1899 over New York that morning giving you my toy soldiers
put away in the attic.

Attic of the Eugene Field House you understand never happened. Remember the *Mary Celeste?* ghost ship abandoned back in 1872 all sails set nobody on board fresh southerly winds a long time ago for such a purpose? Now here is the front page of the *Chicago Tribune* Monday January 4, 1965 The American Paper For Americans:

Tempest Hurls 807 On Ship
Like Ten- pins—16 Hurt in
Nightmare.
The American liner *Independence*—North Atlantic storm—
ripped open a weather door on a
lower deck smashed a porthole
on an upper deck and hurled

half a ton of ice water on a cou-
ple asleep—(presumably waking them)—Captain Riley of the
Independence described the
storm as the worst he had en-
countered in more than 40 years
at sea. "It was like riding a roller coaster."

("By the way, B.J. what ever happened to Forest Park
Highlands?"

"It burned down, boss—hot peep shows in the penny
arcade.")

Well now it so happens that I repatriated myself on the
Independence docked December 8, 1964 if my memory serves I
had the pleasure of meeting Captain Riley at the Captain's
Cocktail Party where no one seemed to know who anybody else
was supposed to be and everybody a bit miffed in consequence.
I approached the Captain directly: "Captain, may I ask you a
question? a *novelist's* question?" (For I was you understand the
distinguished novelist of whom nobody had heard.)

"Why uh yes," he replied guardedly.

"Please tell me Captain quite frankly do you have any theories or guesses in short any shall we say *notions* with regard to
the *Mary Celeste?*"

He replied after a short pause that he could think of no
explanation that accounted for all the facts.

"Captain," I stated firmly "the plain fact is that there are no
facts. I myself—and I may tell you in strictest confidence that I
was once a private investigator—have sifted this matter to the
bottom most deep and established every reason to doubt that
such a ship as the *Mary Celeste* ever existed. The whole thing
was a fabrication out of whole cloth or paper more precisely—
The Captain's Log Book you understand"—and I gave him a
straight look—"Is this the starboard side?" I asked.

"Why yes it is."

"Ah—just so—you see—"

So with the picture of that old sea dog shifting slightly as the ship rolled ports of the world in his eyes and a picture postcard of the SS *Independence* pasted into my own log of the voyage steaming across a paper sea just as empty as the *Mary Celeste*—paper you understand—not a passenger in sight—well just so—"The American paper for Americans—*Independence*—"

So I make these last entries in the log book of my St. Louis return—luggage stacked in the lobby—back through the ruins of Market Street to the Union Station nudes waiting there in the dry fountain of an empty square—I have returned to pick up a few pieces of sunlight and shadow—silver paper in the wind-frayed sounds of a distant city.

VERTIGO OF DEAD LANGUAGES THE
PULLEY AND THE COMPASS LAGOONS
OF MURDEROUS SLEEP-(THEY SHARED
THE *salmon*)-HEAVY STICKY NIGHTS
INKY CLOUDS HAUNTING SHADOWS
COMPASS DRIPPING GEOMETRY...*color*
OF NEW BUILDINGS RINSED BY DOUBT-
(TO SLEEP? NOT TO SLEEP?)-WHITE
NUDITY SLEEPLESS NIGHTS TO THE
GALOP OF WINDOW PANES...ALGEBRA
OF DARKNESS...*erections* IN THE MIR-
RORS OF DRIPPING FACES-(THE SAILORS
ROSE EARLY IN THE URINE OF MEMORY)-
IDA AND MORT VERTIGO OF SHADOWS
SOULLESS WINDED WORDS PANAMA AT
THE WINDOW PEANUTS AND PAREGORIC..
**THERE IS CERTAINLY SOMETHING
WRONG.** *A body split in 2 doesn't know
how to rest..dimmed lights masturbation*
MORNING MIST AGAINST THE WINDOWS.
I WANT TO SEE TOO FAR AWAY THE
HORIZON UNDULATES LIKE SHEET IRON
DISTANCED DILUTED FLESH OF DEAD
MEMORIES FAR OFF SKINS MOTHER
HOUSES MOTHER BODIES. LETTER
MAILED AT SEA CANCELLED WITH WHITE
RUM IN THE SLIME OF PANAMA. PALE
HALO OF *orgasm* SLEEPING ASHES NO-
THING HERE. HERE AFTER LONG
WANDERINGS *frenzied razor slashings
mincemeat of dreams once wounded there is
no rising.* I'LL RETURN ON IDA AND
MORT. LETS NOT TALK ABOUT THE
REST. *MUSE I TELL YOU THAT I STILL
SEE YOU IN A BURST OF FLAMES?* ALL

DELIRIUM IN ASHES ACRID SMOKE *phosherescent rags. Remember, Kid, your new body with parafin added?* LEFTOVERS AT THE 4TH CHIME WALKING WALKING ON ASHES. ONE DIES LIKE THAT DEEP IN THE THROAT. MUST WE SAY THAT THE VENTILATORS ARE STILL THERE FOR A REASON? IT IS MIDNIGHT CIGARETTE AFTER CIGARETTE BLEACHERS OF NAKED FLESH LEFTOVERS..TRAVELER **LEAVE THEM ALONE.** *On the pealed viscera on the bloody sputum* ECHOES OF NOTHING WHISPERED A BACK ROOM.
▣
THE FRISCO KID HE NEVER RETURNS. IN LIFE USED ADDRESS I GIVE YOU. THE WORLD IS NOT MY HOME YOU UNDER- STAND HERE ON YOUNG PEOPLE CRUSHED THROWN FROM A LONG AGO BOY IMAGE MY BONES RETURN TO DUST ADOLESCENT EYES OF ICE BLUE GLASS AND THAT WIND WITH THE *razor.* GOD ANGER. *Memory halves fitted together* THE ATTIC ROOM *lighted cobble stone streets. Slapped the bed: 'Shall we?'* He *led the way through a maze of violet even- ings frayed sounds of distant city peeled his red and white stripped T shirt in the kerosene lamp sputter of burning insect wings.* HE JUMPED WITH HIS KNEES ON THE BED AND SLAPPED HIS THIGHS ASS HAIRS SPREAD OVER THE TIDE FLATS *woke up in other flesh* THE LOOK OUT DIFFERENT *one boy naked in Panama dawn wind. The Frisco Kid he never returns in life used address I give you the world is not my home you understand here on young people. Have you seen Cut City? Have you seen* THE CHIMNEY SWEEPS *take to the*

91

sword? *banner of raw meat live embers ruining in* GUSTS OF FROST. *The eternal watchman rows through the luminous heavens and from his flaming net lets fall shooting stars.* (A flaming hand across the sky DIM JERKY FAR AWAY SOME ONE HAD SHUT A BUREAU DRAWER...*Terrible bright sun hate and hideous hunger in the streets this thing raw peeled dying there in my arms.* YOU **KNEW** HIM SO THAT WAS IT..EITHER WAY IS A BAD MOVE TO THE EAST WING. WHOLE CLUTTER BETTER THAN SHOUTS 'NO GOOD. NO BUENO' NO NO. AND IT IS NO. IT IS CONFUSED AND IT SAYS NO. NOT MUCH TIME LEFT *windy streets flares this long ago address.* A BROKEN SKY BLACKOUT FALLING SAD VOICE CRACKED

   '*Know who I am?*'
HE CAME FRIDAY.

✶
The Frisco Kid he never returns. In life they shared address I give you from a long ago boy adolescent eyes of ice blue glass rinsed by doubt thin white nudity erections in the memory halves fitted together mirrors of dripping faces the attic room lighted. Sailors rose early—urine in cobble stone streets. Mort slapped the bed: 'Shall we?' He led the way through a maze of violet Panama evenings frayed sound of peanuts distant city pealed his red and white striped T shirt morning thighs on the bed ass hairs spread distanced diluted that flesh of dead memories far off one boy naked in Panama dawn wind—(LETTER MAILED AT SEA CANCELLED WITH WHITE RUM IN THE USED ADDRESS) *Remember you new body raw peeled dying there hideous delirium in*

the streets? (My body my arms with parafin
added)- You KNEW him so that was it:
leftovers. Either way is a bad move at the
4th chime walking to the East Wing. Whole
clutter in ASHES. IT IS STILL THERE FOR
A REASON? NOT MUCH TIME IS MIDNIGHT
CIGARETTE AFTER CIGARETTE THIS
LONG AGO ADDRESS *of naked flesh~left-*
overs A BROKEN SKY BLACKOUT FALL-
ING ON THE *peeled viscera on the bloody*
sputum on the sad traveler
'Know who I am? I've come a long way.'
ECHOES OF NOTHING WHISPERED BACK
'HE CAME FRIDAY.'

The Old Movies

"WORD AUTHORITY/MORE HABIT FORMING/THAN HEROIN."

Word authority more habit forming than heroin no this is not the old power addicts talk I am talking about a certain exercise of authority through the use of words authority words habit more forming than heroin that is the use of these words engrams words colorless words form the user more than heroin and he must have more and more heroin authority words more habit than forming that is the words of narcotics control as used by the American Narcotics Dept. more habit forming than can be maintained which is why they must continually spread the problem "authority" more habit forming than word 'heroin' that is the particular authority derived from the enforcement of narcotics laws is more habit forming than the word heroin. What are heroin words? Ally engrams it's going to be all right you are all right and comfortable so comfortable but the words of withdrawal of ally engram is more habit forming than the ally engram notice they need not a few addicts getting it steady they need a lot of addicts always short sick addicts a frequency more habit forming than heroin is the frequency of sick addicts words forming authority in occupation word authority more eristic banal reporters than heroin men of shadows impo- tently flailing anachronic consensus nevermore addict talk bubbling about a certain uxorious urubu beneath innavigable umlaut of authority dim words ukase over decorticated canines jerky pretext colorless tin far away habit heroin's logomachy supine societal eschatology infra sound called these words engram words colorless words form the user's canine perspec- tives word authority more habit forming latterly endemic than heroin anachronic experiments with blue infrasound I am talk- ing established drug authority about a certain irrefrangible exercise of authority through necessities ill informed pulp of words that is the particular authority banal reporter's camera derived from enforcement men of shadows anachronic narcot- ics laws more habit forming than preparations bubbling 'heroin' beneath innavigable umlaut shallow and unworthy what are heroin words? dim ally engrams colorless far away

and comfortable so comfortable canine dance floor flickering
latterly endemic American friend feeding canine preparation
the Countess Repulsive obligatory blue bubbling about a certain uxorious urubu investiture died when their batteries on
sham rage enforcement men of shadows he enjoys quality job
gave out you're fired by any reputably informed obmutesence
his young eyes narrowed to grey slits ... authority deadlier
than cocaine he must have more and more ... battle a pretext
thin hero words colorless dim words I am sure control machine
ukase over decorticated canine preparations lighted length of
time I am talking about a certain irrefrangible authority the
torn palatogram fell into our hands pretty baby please engram
words colorless flower flesh inert words engram words form the
user obligatory have more and more from the users abrasively
incondite control ... you're fired endemic encumbrancer the
clock has stopped old urubu on the darkened 23rd hour the
golden stars flailing they must continually incubus's interposi-
tional contagonist spread the problem word 'heroin' justiciar
congruent that is the particular authority congruently flailing
latterly endemic derived from enforcement of decommissioned
encumbrancer's anachronic narcotics laws habit forming
flower flesh shadow ally obligatory obscurant effluvial notice
they need not a few addicts epidemically obligatory such investiture a frequency more habit forming abrasively incondite
than heroin is immeasurably impacted endemic encumbrancer's uxorious frequency of sick addicts incubus's word
forming authority's prefigured eschatologist decommissioned
externalized investiture shallow and unworthy.

From SO WHO OWNS DEATH TV

A boy as quoted in *The Desperate Years* assembled by James D. Horan ... 'A boy has never wept nor dashed a thousand. Kim, did you hear me? Henry, Max, come over hear. French Canadian, bean soup. I want to pay. Let them leave me alone. These are a few quotations but it goes on for several pages. I have made many variations and cut ins with the Dutchman of which here are a few samples: 'Let me in the district boy. I want to pay. Those dirty rats have tuned in the treatment works. Grystal proportions the dose. I even get it from the department Great Eastern Blizzard 1888 by his pipe—overhead light— left—B. Brainard one man show and why did I kill him? who shot you? *Quien es?* He was one of the people responsible for introducing the trap heal. He was a cowboy in one of the seven days a week fight no and it is no buttons. it is confused and it says no ... This waxen clinging mouth and chains—*disguise en?*—what dies in *color? your name? Remember who shot you?* Blue Star me for very uncleanly spirit ... rot wrapped February 6 is my birthday ... I am going to give you Panama *consumption / cough* / blackout falling—No? and it is no buttons. Then the shooting starts—the nabor has photo like you and me but graphed a cat on the balcony ... no there's handcuffs on them. The fine Greek hand signing phantom injury ... yes he's fruitful—the Baron says these things *angeblich—ich sterbe*—they were drafter ... —Just get those dirty Panama pictures out of here—Hurry up please it is war everywhere—Have you met the Skipper yet? storms / cracklin sounds / the noises first and then the lights / laser / guns / the whole sky? do you hear me, Kim? Kim! Nova! The chimney sweeps take to the sword. Explorers moving in whole armies and he sets me fishing lark. So that boy decided to go out in May. Have you met Fort Charles skipper yet? He was presumed in army special to the new drowned after his motor boat the St. Foreigner was found beached and empty at Ohio Ticker rumors Cleveland. About face journals last days.

(Do you have a gram?)

There it is just everything dumdum weather report ahead—
red brick house in Sunday best—Corner Magical *Alley*—Well
yeah cook it with *the orphanage* parsley—jacking off order
O.K. *telescope you can watch the boys surface in jissom*—I'm
waiting *jacking off* on the corner—the dormitory a haunted
ruin you understand toppled into the river—There was the
consul decided something well odd about the pale faded eyes
that seemed to be looking at some distant *lavendar horizon and
the priest's face long ago* . . . report me next—I hated socks and
in Sunday best—well yeah later at Oak St.—you're still
parsley—*Jacking off order O.K. there, 867 Golden Gate? Con-
stituting a frozen vibrating smoke erection shoes albatross*—
Calling Ida Mol and Mort—Bill Gray, my tape connection is
broken—NOVA POLICE Tiburon Island—child memories are
4 P.M. Alesbury Road—spirits on sporadic location—the *new
growth that orgasm octopus spread out on terrible youth—back
to the* recording tape—Albatross calling—(Do you love me?)—
the summer porch—hardens—mouth to mouth smokes—*my
whole protosubstance bended to years ago sporadic Clayton
Street scene*—undercover agent—old school ties—I am BZ
008—let's go *fuzzy*—blue 6 and my name is John—(his masturbation name was John) dead hand *jacking off scar tissue—
flesh—emergency exit—about here on young people—frayed
thing of scar tissue 4 P.M. faded pink neither alive nor dead—
sad old man of 20 very stagnant flowers—si me quieres flesh
diseased burnt out inside? The orgasm octopus spread out raw
peeled dying there—slow masturbation used to be me Mister —*

Meet me in the shooting gallery stop quiet the roses stop ship scenes necessary stop D & D Who? Don't be tiresome. Inspector Hugh is the flabbiest hope this reaches you time dilation before after it is obvious on the beach/ Please adjust your brakes, Johnny Cool the Manola Section. last beach quick sand. It is dangerous to swim from Phallus 3 standing with the arrival of bubbles. What were you doing at Billgray's Trop ice? Signed Mort, Uncle Jim, Flower, Dawn, Blue Kid, C.P. Taylor, San Francisco 9. Beach Alignments clear eucalyptus leaves (re: Three Came To Conquer) flutes of sperm mouth to mouth smokes rose sunset memories warm greenish sky blazing fresh gestures out of smoke East Beach, are you a member of the union? Film Union 17? East Beach shall I phone Friendly Gray Post? ... deadline.nothing or dare lot. You like furniture more than signal towers;;mate?

Random Group MU Paris, J.R. (soto steele group t.Milano) B.G. shaping Big Picture silent sunday to 1st. I. O.U. disk unfolders a blue print in the Boy's Mag rusty lasergun there windy street half buried in sand transitory halting place Hi, Bill, Dixie Land, Pantopon Rose? How's things with you? Cold coffee sitting right where you care sitting now a chair that folds. I picked up my little bag and walked into the Missouri night stopping over the ashes. Find out now the world is dead? Tell me again? T.V. (T.B.) agony to breathe here. Mist falls like parachutes on the moon Rescape 7 (sharp smell of weeds from old Westerns) white cockatoo made in China reading reliable gun shots. Stand in for Mr. WHO? Captain Clark welcomes you aboard. Set your clocks forward an hour. Calm English Miracle APO-MORPHINE smile welcomes you temperate climate and brussel sprouts room with rose wallpaper made the bed and went out six? seven? P.M. lights on in the pub across the street?

Are you a member of the union? Film Union 4 P.M. Don't seem to remember receiving your union dues old boy. You poka me late afternoon change without shadows on the wall do not be surprised if the old sunlight in his voice is short You can guess what trivia chickens squawking outside are there cigarette please take a cup of tea up to the workman on the roof did you buy eat food cat? remote foreign suburbs the cock crows gray sultry afternoon what a spot to land with a crippled ship. End of a subdivision St. Agony to breathe here. 19th Wallgreens on the dead burnt out face. 1st hell here waiting on the corner of Magical St. You are alone in the world last junky selling his empty suitcase distant 1920 wind and dust. Come, Kid, photo flip *gun shots*. Towers Open Fire a long time ago. (smoke shreds of phosphorescent flesh. Sharky's word film dimmer far away his shark skin sleeve) beat whistling in the harbor cuts his voice.

I am right. you are wrong.
. ”   *   :   +   @
you are wrong. I am right.
:   +   @   . ”   *
I am right? you are wrong.
. ”   *   :   +   @
you are wrong? I am right.
:   +   @   . ”   *
I am cop kicks in door right flashes his dirty rotten
.   ”
hunkatin you dragged away in handcuffs are wrong man
*   :   +   @
has cornered a rat I am he raises a heavy stick right
                    @   ”   *
you the rat gives a squeak of terror are the rat bares
:   +
his yellow teeth wrong stick falls dying rat twitches I
+   @
am right cop clubs man in riot scene you are he kicks
.   ”   *   :
him into the wagon wrong he slams door I am executioner
              +   @   .
enters death cell right with two guards you come along
”   **   :
are strapped into electric chair wrong smoke curls up
                              +
from electrodes 'I pronounce this man dead' wrong
                                            @
Harry S. Truman decides to drop first atom bomb I
.   ”   *
am right you people in Hiroshima are wrong film shows
:   +
burned children I am cop breaks through door 'I am
@   .   ”
a police officer right enough.' mixed time and place
*   *   :
he was looking for a teen age drug party. He has

strayed into Dillinger's hideout you are Dillinger

102

covers him with submachine gun wrong copper raised
    +
hands terror I am right he holds gun on cop's stomach
    @   .   "   *
1914 movie two men arguing outside bar coats off I am

right man 1 knocks man 2 down you are wrong man 2
              .   "   *   :   +   @   .
gets up I am right he throws right to jaw sequence
    "   *
repeated up down fade out The End. The general is

making a difficult decision in the Pentagon dim jerky
                                   "
far away he paces up and down the office buries his

face in his hands he looks up at the American flag he
                                                *
picks up phone you are wrong Commies atom bombs
        :
fall on Moscow Moscow in ruins I am right counter
        +   @
missiles whistle you are wrong Pentagon blows up
    "   *   :   +
mushroom cloud
    @
Am I right? you are wrong.
"   .   *   :   +   @
Are you wrong? right I am.
+   :   @   *   .   "
Right I am. Wrong you are.
*   .   "   @   :   +
Right? Wrong? I am? Are you?
*   @   .   "   +   :
Right our wrong: I am you.
*   +   @   .   "   :
Wrong are you right? I am.
@   +   :   *   .   "

103

I am you right or wrong.
.   ”   :   *   +   @
Wrong you are. I write. Am.
  @   :   +   .   *   ”
I write you are wrong. Am
.   *   :   +   @   ”
Wrong eye am right? you? our?
  @   .   ”   *   :   +
Our right eye am wrong you.
+   *   .   ”   @   :
Right or wrong you am I.
   *   +   @   :   ”   .
Am wrong right? you are I?
”   @   *   :   + .
I   am   right   youarewrongwrongwrongIIIamamamamright
.   ”   *   :   +   @   @   @   ...   ”   ”   ”   ”   *
rightrightyouyouyouyou areareourorareareourwrongyou
   *   *   :   :   :   : + + + + + +   @   :
orrightamIIIrightamorwrongyou
+   *   ”   ..   *   ”   +   @   :
.”*:+@.....”””””””*****:::::+++++@@@@@*:*:*....”.”.

”...@:@:@:@:@:****”””””:@@@:@:@:@:@.......:@:@:@:

:@ ::”:”::”””:*@ *@ “@ “@ “@ “@ “@ .*.*.*.*..”.”:”:”.

”.”...:..::”::@:@@:@*@*@”@”@@@”””*””++*+*+*+

+”+”+++”+”:”:”:”...@.@.@.@.....+@+@+@+@+@

+@.....*:”.+”+@.@.:@+@+@+@+@+++”++*++”.

””.:@:::@++@+++@+++*::”::”+”++””±”@”@””@@:

:@..@:@.@+@+@@++”++*+*++”++”:”...::*:*:”:”:”

:@:@+@+@@.@..@++@...@::::@..@:@:”:”:*:*:....::::

:++++....*.*..@.@.@..@:@:::.::.@:.@++@+”+”+”+”+

Breaks through door Im a poli flashes his dirty rotten
                        "
hunka tin time and place he was looking for are wrong
     *
he puts the cuffs on? he has strayed into Dillinger's
                    ?
right stick him with sub machine gun wrong cop rat
                         *
bares his yellow teeth detective knocks man to floor
     +
if you are gay I am right seconds with Karate you are
                                      *
wrong you are he kicks him into 1914 movie outside bar

coats off Harry S. Truman decides to drop first you
                            "
are wrong Hiroshima wrong film of right to jaw
          +   *
sequence repeat child I am executioner is making a
                ?
difficult decision you come along strapped into head
         "
electrodes I am cop kicks in the door right officer
                      .   "   *
right enough mixed you he sticks a gun in a teen age
              :
drug party cornered rat I am right noise man kills
  ?   *
him in 30 seconds detective dying I am right right
                              ?
Harry 2 gets up I am right he throws atom bomb I am
     .   "   *
right you people in Hiroshima survivors burned the
       :   +
Pentagon dim jerky far away smoke. □
   ?   *

ABSTRACT

Doktor Kurt Unruh von Steinplatz writes: "He who opposes force alone forms that which he opposes and is formed by it"... (Film shows Tzarist secret police using same interrogation methods as GPU)... On the other hand he who does not resist force that enslaves and exterminates will be enslaved and exterminated... (Film shows extermination of Bushmen, Australian aborigines, American Indians)... "For revolution to effect basic change in existing conditions three tactics are required: 1. Disrupt. 2. Attack. 3. Disappear. Look away. Ignore. Forget." Accordingly he enunciated the concept of My Own Business, units consisting of like-minded individuals forming separate communities: "These communities must be camouflaged to survive." (MOB takes over apartment building from mortgage to janitor. Now another next door. Now a whole block on the surface normal everyday stupid folk. MOB takes over small town bank jail and sheriff. No beards no long hair. Just an ordinary small town)... "New concepts can only arise when one achieves a measure of disengagement from enemy conditions. On the other hand disengagement is difficult in a concentration camp is it not?... Disrupt: Fifty young men record riot sound effects on portable tape recorders. Recorders are placed in identical brief cases. They dust identical grey flannel suits lightly with tear gas. They hit the rush hour recorders on full blast... screams, police whistles, breaking glass, crunch of night sticks, tear gas flapping from their clothes. Attack in subsequent confusion. Retire to MOB. Disappear. Look away. Ignore. Forget."

Birth death the human condition... Women will always hear the children... "Hello Ma," said the astronaut.

Laboratory where scientists are working to develop vaccines and anti-virus agents. The scientists look at their watches. It is time to shift sets.

Same scientists work for that crazy American government to develop visionary strains of fulminating vaccine-resistant virus. Scientist holds up a chicken egg with a tiny pinhole thru which we see Medieval epidemics . . . "Bring out your dead." The film speeds up. Scientists rush back and forth from one laboratory to the other. Finally a scientist is making *interferon* with one hand and malignant hepatitis with the other.

"Newspapers are largely responsible for the dreary events they describe. It is recommended that all daily papers be discontinued" . . . Academy Bulletin 235.

Audrey writes: "The last carnival is being pulled down, buildings and stars laid flat for storage . . . fading streets a distant sky . . . old photos melted into air."

City editor bellows: "Go out and get those pictures." . . . Click Negro burned alive in Omaha . . . Click Negro lynched in Mississippi . . . Click execution of Ruth Snyder . . . Click Tokyo earthquake . . . Click Halifax explosion . . . Click Hiroshima.

Postscript to "The Invisible Generation":

As I have indicated in "The Invisible Generation" (published in *The Los Angeles Free Press* and also as a postscript in *The Ticket That Exploded)* a technique for producing events and directing thought on a mass scale is available to anyone with a portable tape recorder or a car to transport recorders. The basis for this technique is waking suggestion first used by Doctor John Dent of London who also introduced the apomorphine treatment for drug addiction and alcoholism.

Waking suggestion as practiced by Dr. Dent: The patient is instructed to read aloud from a book while concentrating his attention on what he is reading as if reading to an imaginary person seated in front of him. The doctor stands behind him and repeats at the same voice level the patient is using certain suggestions previously agreed upon between doctor and patient ("You will be able to sleep," "You will not relapse into the use of alcohol," etc.). The patient, since he is reading aloud and his attention is concentrated on what he is reading, does not hear the suggestions consciously and for this reason they take a different effect on his subconscious or reactive mind. *This is not subliminal suggestion.* Subliminal means below the level of conscious sight or hearing. Even if the subject were concentrating all his attention on the source of subliminal sounds or images he would not be able to see or hear anything. Waking suggestion consists of sounds or images which are not consciously registered *since the subject's attention is else-where.* If his attention were directed towards the source he would be able to see or hear it immediately. Waking suggestion not subliminal suggestion is the technique used in playback of pre-recorded tapes in the street, cocktail parties, bars, stations, airports, parks, subways, political rallies, theater intermissions, etc. People do not consciously hear the taped suggestions because their attention is directed towards something else: Crossing street, catching train, listening for plane call, listening to speaker, looking at TV, talking to companions. The volume of the tape is adjusted to street sounds, speech level and so forth. A well-constructed suggestion tape will have pre-recorded street sounds or whatever cut in according to location.

Any suggestion tape is made much more effective if it contains contradictory commands. Stop. Go. Wait here. Go there. Come in. Stay out. Be a man. Be a woman. Be white. Be black. Live. Die. Be a human animal. Be a superman. Yes. No. Do it now. Do it later. Be your real self. Be somebody else. Rebel. Submit. RIGHT. WRONG. Make a splendid impression. Make an awful impression. Sit down. Stand up. Take your hat off. Put your hat on. Create. Destroy. React. Ignore. Live now. Live in the past. Live in the future. Obey the law. Break the law. Be ambitious. Be modest. Accept. Reject. Do more. Do less. Plan ahead. Be spontaneous. Decide for yourself. Listen to others. Talk. SILENCE. Save money. Spend money. Speed up. Slow down. This way. That way. Right. Left. Present. Absent. Open. Closed. Up. Down. Entrance. Exit. IN. OUT.

These commands are constantly being imposed by the environment of modern life. If, for example, your suggestion tape contains the phrase "Look at that light in front of you ... STOP ... Stay here ... GO ... Be over there" ... and is played back to people waiting at a stop light *they are forced to obey the sugges-*

tion you are making. It's like giving someone a sleeping pill without his knowledge and then suggesting sleep. And any contradictory suggestion at the unconscious level produces a moment of disorientation during which your suggestions take effect. Furthermore, contradictory suggestions are an integral function of human metabolism . . . "Sweat. Stop sweating. Salivate. Stop salivating. Pour adrenalin into the bloodstream. Counteract adrenalin." Since contradictory commands are enforced by the environment and by the human body, suggestion tapes that contain such commands are especially effective. All tape recorder tricks are useful: speed up, slow down, overlay running contradictory commands simultaneously, echo chambers for stations and airports. Effects are obtained by persistence and exposure—by getting as many operators in the street as possible. For wide coverage use a car cutting-in your suggestions with popular tunes and street sounds. When playing back insult tapes the operator is well advised to move fast and stay out of his wake.

August 1978

This text arranged in my New York loft, which is the converted locker room of an old YMCA. Guests have reported the presence of a ghost boy. So this is a Oui-Ja board poem taken from *Dumb Instrument*, a book of poems by Denton Welch, and spells and invocations from the *Necronomicon*, a highly secret magical text released in paperback. There is a pinch of Rimbaud, a dash of St.-John Perse, an oblique reference to *Toby Tyler with the Circus*, and the death of his pet monkey.

FEAR AND THE MONKEY

Turgid itch and the perfume of death
On a whispering south wind
A smell of abyss and of nothingness
Dark Angel of the wanderers howls through the loft
With sick smelling sleep
Morning dream of a lost monkey
Born and muffled under old whimsies
With rose leaves in closed jars
Fear and the monkey
Sour taste of green fruit in the dawn
The air milky and spiced with the trade winds
White flesh was showing
His jeans were so old
Leg shadows by the sea
Morning light
On the sky light of a little shop
On the odor of cheap wine in the sailors' quarter
On the fountain sobbing in the police courtyards
On the statue of moldy stone
On the little boy whistling to stray dogs.

Wanderers cling to their fading home
A lost train whistle wan and muffled
In the loft night taste of water
Morning light on milky flesh
Turgid itch ghost hand
Sad as the death of monkeys
Thy father a falling star
Crystal bone into thin air
Night sky
Dispersal and emptiness.

DISTANT HEELS

In the noon streets a crowd was gathering quick silent hate blazing something cracked in his head like a red egg and he was running toward them up the narrow street moving his head from side to side burning a path thru charred flesh and shredded brains. He was clear now running very light on his feet up the steep stone street towards the film skies of Marrakesh the whole film tilting now the stone moving in waves under his feet a blaze of blue in his head engulfed him held him upright stabbing two black holes in the blue sky smoking with a sound like falling mountains the sky ripped open and he was thru the film barrier a heavy medium his movements very slow the words in his mind slowed down and flowed away on a grey river vibrating in slow oscillations his body losing outline he could move freely now looking down at a naked adolescent body in a dim attic silent film he couldn't talk there were no words in his mind standing naked in front of a wash stand with a picture of hot water looked like copper lustre but there was no colour in this world only light and shadow.

The film jumped and shifted music across the golf course he was a caddy it seems looking for lost balls by the pond music from the country club fireflies winking spots of light room over the florist shop flickering silver buttocks in the dark room smell of young night he was coming sad furtive hand suburban toilet smell of semen fading flickering the film jerky stops in stills back through family portraits to 1870 streets of Paris words again but different the words were there when he wanted them not all the time the people he passed seemed possessed of some superhuman secret of equanimity but looking closer he saw that they were just ordinary people shopkeepers business men by finding that area again he had shattered the structure of reality all from an old movie will give at his touch.

When I describe events and people as a film I mean it quite literally a talking film of you round the clock doing what you are doing urinating defecating sitting on the Terrace of the Glacier reading *Le Petit Marocain* modest little paper ejaculat-

ing dreaming and the yellow blue awakening purple fogs in the evening vodka tonic the soundtrack muttering away in your head unanswered letters the rent to pay on the flat in London you see how the film keeps you talking away and dictates what you will say film garbage on the doorstep what the hell is this
"FATIMA"
and so on what you say all day there's a Coca Cola sign you say Coca Cola right enough splice your film in with someone else's film he picks up your mutter and sees things different the look-out different. I am the Director it's a sick picture boss cut off surrounded gun empty these foreign shit-birds here in a grade B movie production Maroc at night he dreamed of escape someone knocking at the door stale hung over I smoke too much
"FATIMA S'IL VOUS PLAIT"
You notice the only time you felt free alone in your room with my old sergeant hash as soon as you have to move you have to talk try getting to the corner without talking your way there on my film. Do you begin to see there is no corner there? Reggie through the door with his briefcase the boy comes at four must go to Tangier soon Reggie in the courtyard
"FATIMA CHANGEZ MON LIT"
rehearsing what I will say to the boy who has asked me to pay his way to Germany the whole film flat and dead I must go to Tangier in a few days they have shut off our electricity a boy downstairs talking to Farid I can't hold this post much longer raw pealed dying in the noon streets
"Good evening you very nice man"
open door a beggar throw the gasoline on them and light it quick hate and hunger in the streets every day uglier more hopeless no relief in sight desperate agents trying to escape from the film they know how it ends terrible I've seen it rags of dead green flesh as the film buckled and ebbed leaking the great lover in noon streets of Marrakesh it could happen here any time the film sky buckles terrible sickness of dead flesh long dead kept alive in film when it hits people go mad for a purpose any purpose to hold them together or you leak from here to the corner.

He had a round room and when you opened the door the room

was like a cool well on his naked body.

And there he is again some day later across the street and no dice flickered across his face smiled around the corner the date is right blurred 1920s so long ago the old grey corner younger his body I looked back about 19 sadness in his eyes the corner shop I was walking behind him at the corner I turn down the old Rider Street lost 19 just say something one word and no dice flickered across his good bye children shoes I could touch almost his mouth a little open looking for a name difficulty rather ambiguous voices couldn't find the microwaves last figure 8 looks like the young thief used to be the Lex Garage down Brewer Street it is getting dark boy burglar spots the door open wooden benches inside he is calling what used to be many years ago the shop boy solid his mouth a little open mutters at the door.

"Abrupt question brought me meester . . ." Desolate thin blue overcoat far to go . . . a street sadness in his eyes shop door looking for a name . . . click of distant heels

"Any suggestions Rogers?"

"Well, surely headquarters must see the value in this project. Why hang it all? The possibilities are unlimited. We'll get it around among the Commies . . . Mix it in a candybar or soft drink maybe." The Chief's eyes were cold. "And when they get it well spread around they won't need someone to pick up the tab."

"Well, if everyone was on our product and we had an exclusive on the distribution . . ."

"Everybody isn't on our product. Two out of three on the first experiment. That isn't enough. I tell you the whole thing could blow up in our faces. One doctor is all it takes. One wisecracker putting cases together . . . Sure, I know doctors are encouraged . . . you know how encouraging *we* can be by reporting addicts at once. In one day we got two thousand reported. Somebody doesn't start asking questions? Our erstwhile friends on the Press begin to talk: "America must face the solemn truth that some of our most trusted public servants have betrayed the trust invested in them."

They walked to the Djemma el Fna. They sat on the terrace of the Glacier. Reggie got out of a taxi with a suitcase, a walking corpse muttering under film skies of Marrakesh.

PAGES FROM CHAOS

The scouting party stopped a few hundred yards from the village on the bank of a stream. Yen Lee studied the village thru his field glasses while his men sat down and lit cigarettes. The village was built into the side of a mountain. The stream ran thru the town and the water had been diverted into pools on a series of cultivated terraces that led up to the monastery. There was no sign of life in the steep winding streets or by the pools. Evidently word of the scouting party had reached the villagers and they were shut up in their stone houses. He lowered his glasses, signaling to the men to follow cautiously. The valley was littered with large boulders which would serve as cover if necessary, but he did not expect resistance on a military level. The men crossed a stone bridge two at a time, covered by the men behind them. If any defenders were going to open fire this would be the time and place to do it. Beyond the bridge a street twisted up the mountainside. On both sides there were stone huts, fallen to ruins and obviously deserted. As they moved up the stone street, keeping to the sides and taking cover behind the ruined huts, Yen Lee became increasingly aware of a hideous unknown odor. He motioned to the patrol to halt and stood there sniffing. Rotten ozone was his tentative classification.

Unlike his official counterparts in Western countries, he had been carefully selected for a high level of intuitive adjustment and trained accordingly to imagine and explore seemingly fantastic potentials in any situation, while at the same time giving equal consideration to prosaic and practical aspects. His training had given him an attitude at once probing and impersonal, remote and alert. He did not know when the training had begun, since training in Academy 23 was carried out in a context of reality. He did not see his teachers and their instructions were conveyed through a series of real situations. He had been born in Hong Kong and had lived there until the age of 12, so that English was a second language. Then his family had moved to Shanghai. In his early teens he had read the American Beat writers, the volumes having been brought in through Hong Kong and sold under the counter in a book-shop that seemed to enjoy freedom from official interference, although the proprietor was also engaged in currency deals. At the age of 16 he was sent to a military academy, where he received intensive training in the use of weapons. After six months he was summoned to the colonel's office and told that he would be leaving the military school and returned to Shanghai. Since he had applied himself to the training and made an excellent showing he asked if this was because his work had not been satisfactory. The colonel was not looking at him but around him, as if drawing a figure in the air. He indicated obliquely that while a desire to please one's superiors was laudable other considerations were in certain cases even more urgently emphasized.

And then the smell hit him like an invisible wall. He stopped and leaned against a house. It was like rotten metal or metal excrement he decided. The patrol was still on the outskirts of the village. One man was vomiting violently. Yen Lee filled a syringe with an anti-nausea drug and gave the man an injection. The others helped the sick man to the stream.

"Don't drink the water," Yen Lee ordered. "The stream runs through the town."

He sat down and lit a cigarette, and then looked once again at the town through his field glasses. There were still no villagers in sight, but he knew they were there. He could feel the eyes through the stone walls of the village. He smiled briefly, wishing that another of the cadets was with him on the patrol. His men were soldiers, and good ones, but that was all. They had not received the special training that he had been through. An exercise he remembered at the military academy had been to pose a difficult situation to a cadet and tell him to write several possible ways out, illustrating each with photographs. Had he been living in England or America he could have been a successful writer. But writing was only a part of his training.

Now he put the glasses down and made an imaginary exploration of the village... what "they," he thought, would call "astral travel." He was moving up the street now. He kicked open a door. He spoke Tibetan of course, but one glance at the prisoner told him that interrogation was useless. At least he would get no information on the verbal level. The man was literally sub-normal and in the terminal stages of some disease, his face eaten by phosphorescent scars. Then Yen Lee advanced to the monastery itself, his men spread out for cover, their weapons ready. Then he stopped; his training had not quite prepared him for the feeling of death that fell like a steady silent rain from the monastery above him. He lit another cigarette. Exploration had drawn a blank and he knew only what he had already surmised, that the monastery contained some force, possibly radioactive. The men were equipped with gas masks. He could of course make a preliminary reconnaissance of the village, or they could scale the mountain and get above the monastery, but it would be hazardous and time-consuming. He picked up his walkie-talkie.

"Pre-talk calling Dead-line."

"Well?" The colonel's voice was cool, edged with an abstract impatience. The cadets were expected to use their own initiative on patrol and only call in case of emergency.

"Outskirts of the city. Can't get through. The smell alone would drop a vulture at five hundred yards."

"Did you expect a summer golf course? You have masks!"

"Well, there is something else here. The death feeling. Can't get through it. . . .

23 SKIDDOO

I work for the 23 Screwball Department. We got our files on all nut cases and each case is classified like 23.: could write a threatening letter or slither an unloaded blank cartridge pistol at a queen if we nerved him up to it definitely not 23 . . . : : : that is assassin timber now for that the old reliable is the quiet type read the bible kept to himself far away look in his eyes it was a dreamy look and at the same time it was a disagreeable look but nobody liked to look at it so it passed unnoticed until one day just as the Consul got out of his car at 10.23 A.M. he was amazed to be approached by what he took to be an uncouth beggar carrying a bible in one hand and in the other what later turned out when extracted from the Consul's spine after repeatedly penetrating his liver and abdomen to be an eight inch boning knife. As he struck the assassin was heard to say: "After all God made knives."

Overpowered by consular guards and turned over to the police the assassin admitted to being a member of the "Fly Tox Movement" an extremist sect who hold hashish in horror getting their kicks largely from vitamin deficiency a preparation like that you can get on his line sweet and clear.

"Can you hear me Homer? Of course you can. I'm telling you what you have to do Homer. We will protect you Homer. Flying saucers will be waiting after you have done our bidding."

Now it sometimes happens you lose a screwball can't get on his line well then you put everybody with cop in him out on the streets to trace down the lost screwball before he talks too sensible about what we are doing here in this department which is unthinkable because we got here first heavy and cold as a cop's blackjack on a winter night we was looking for a lost screwball last contacted in an orgone accumulator screen went dead case like that usually turns out to be inter-departmental sabotage or illegal recruitment the whole department is rotten with it maybe the Ethnology Department used him in a ritual murder we are men of the world these things happen . . .

"Joe may my flesh rot if this department knows what you are talking about." Right through the departments cold hate of a questioned accountant who knows his books are right. We had to face the possibility our ball had been nutnipped and might be used to exterminate one of our own white haired boys like the Old Sugar Boss.

At the office party Mr. Blankslip from accounting mixed his "blackout special" and a little cold voice told him this man must be killed to save the Lamb of God from the Beast 666 as a member of the special squadron your duty is clear comrade a man has his simple job to do for Total Oil the company always takes care of its own you didn't think I'd let you down son? God? Well not exactly just a plain Joe with a job to do like you've got a job to do now faced by the unspeakable Old Sugar Boss after three martinis letting his co-workers he calls us know we are all jolly decent plain Joes like him he had a slimy way say if a member of the staff came into the office without his shoes shined the boss would stop having his own shoes shined and call attention to it at all times receiving a foreign dignatory apologized for the state of his shoes "as a matter of office procedure you understand" until you got the hint and came in with your shoes like obsidian mirrors and the boss smiles slow like stiff molasses and says "Good to see you" or he would leave a small sum of money out on the desk then pinch it himself most likely

"Oh uh Grimsy?"

"Yes sir"

"You didn't happen to see fifteen shillings on my desk did you? Thought you might have put it in petty cash? No? Lying right there on the desk..."

"I didn't see it sir."

"Well it's not important... Good night Grimsy..."

"Good night sir."

"Oh.. Grimsy..."

"Yes sir."

"If you need an advance on your salary you can ask for it you know..."

He had a way of dropping in on his staff at any time no staff member was permitted to have locks on his doors not even the bathroom any hour of the day or night the Old Sugar Boss throws your door open and smiles at you.

"Well writing late in our diary? That must make interesting reading."

One morning his car blew up the explosion flattening a city block. Clearly O.I.—Outside Influence—is at work. Whole sections of the machine are now riddled and clogged by what the Party Chairman termed "Cod eyed Communist buffoons who are sabotaging important projects." We must trace down all cases of lost contact though like I say most of them turn out to be inter-departmental louse ups you get in a creep outfit like this but you never know when a lost ball has fallen under O.I. until the damage is done. When you see their ball my friend it is too late.

"Get your hands off me you filthy old bum!"

Just so happens empty street doorman around the corner for a "rouge" ... bleeding profusely he was carried into the lobby where he described his assailant as "wearing a light blue suit stained down the front with scrambled eggs and smelling abominably of raw onions and cheap spirits." The attacker had disappeared.

"To be used again in some other garb of course."

My superior nodded "Some old nut with pamphlets. You attempt to brush by him ..."

O.I. could screw up our whole department since we have now perfected and demonstrated in the filed operation Mass 23 Skiddoo ...::: Indonesia ::: ... induced by computerized techniques in otherwise normal population a leak at this stage is simply unthinkable it could unthink the whole department preoccupied with these thoughts he was amazed to be stopped rather roughly by a gendarme

"See here I'm from the Ministry of Interior" He glanced sharply at the agent "Why that uniform is a fake."

He looked around for a proper cop and died without regaining consciousness. The assassin, described by police as "the professional brother of a cop" said the Under Secretary made a threatening gesture and he fired in self defense. Day like another quiet American eating scrambled eggs in Needicks suddenly the

Philippino cook came from behind the counter moving with a strangely purposeful trot...

"New man on the job ... eager to please" the quiet American thought. He smiled warmly "Warm my eggs up will you Jojo?"

Cold eggs cold coffee cold American on the floor

"Hello senor you like my country yes?"

"Why sure Mother and me both love Mexico. Won't you join us in a beer?"

"Two gringos more or less between machos I was crudo"

Her first thought was she must have left something in Lips and this horrid young man in a black leather jacket was running out to give it to her she was much too rich to tip him but what was that in his hand exactly? The grenade blew her mink coat fifty yards.

Man he thought was a new doorman barring his way to the Yale Club suddenly produced a bottle dowsed him with gasoline and set him on fire. You never know when damage is done for that old reliable is late and an orgone accumulator screen went dead on a winter night like that usually turns out screen went dead and the whole department is illegal Mr. Blankslip mixed his black out Lamb of God from the Beast 666 now faced by the unspeakable Ethnology Department all his co-workers he calls us know these things happen by Joes like him he had a slimy way say of talking right through my flesh Old Sugar Boss after three martinis

"We are all jolly decent plain Joes slob clear."

Grenade .. anteroom of the consulate a new doorman barring his way light blue suit stained down the front dowsed with gasoline was crudo a gendarme stopped him rather roughly

"Won't you have a beer?"

Regaining consciousness assassins stalk the passer by and all brothers of a cop said Swedish Consul quietly eating scrambled eggs in Needicks ... Oswalds and Rubys were but plates dropped from our pockets human time bombs exploded on computerized order. Now all precision is lost random assassins and buffoons prowl the street and all this anarchy resulted from one lost ball.

And who do you think was the first agent on the golf course? Quite by chance the same stranger here? After all I am 23 ...::::

OLD PHOTOGRAPHER

An old man sits in a 1920 Spanish study a bit of tapestry on the stucco walls that arch to a vaulted ceiling. On the desk of black oak in front of him is a cobra lamp. The old man is covered by a silver sheen here and there holes in his film through which show the leather backs of the *Encyclopedia Britannica.*

"Old photographer trick, young man ... smile see the birdie ... well, the subject freezes ... So I figured if I put on a loud click *after* I took the picture maybe I would get better pictures ... like when they hear the click I already took the picture say 10 seconds ago. Result was the face more frozen than ever. Why? Because the face is moving. You never take a picture of the present but always of the future. In short, if you want a picture of how someone looks when the shutter clicks you take a picture a few seconds before the shutter clicks. Now this was just what I didn't want then since I was young and I wanted good pictures. That was long long ago. I didn't know it but I already knew too much. Oh yes I found out how to get my good pictures and made a lot of money as a portrait photographer. All I had to do was find out what words music picture odor brought out in the subject the face I wanted. Then I took my picture just *before* I played the music or whatever the cue was and the subject never knew when the picture was taken since I still used the false click gimmick. Reaction time? Yes, I went into that. You see, I couldn't just pick up the money and forget it. Better if I had. I was warned. But I couldn't get it out of my mind. And I found the answer: allowing for reaction time there was still an interval of a few seconds unaccounted for ... I was taking a picture not of the face as it is 'now' but as it would be in a few seconds: I was photographing the future. Those words crossed my mind in silver letters. Then old Fred Flash came to call, sitting right where you are sitting now: 'Well my boy, you have put your foot in it now. You see, people are never paid not to reveal what they know. They are paid not to find something out. We tried to pay you. Just look at this house: modern, convenient .. you find it so, of course .. Well, you wouldn't just pick up our money and go back to your stamp collection. Oh no: you had to know. All right, so now you know. All right you can take over my job now ...' Old Fred Flash ... I take all the pictures. I take the first picture and I take the last picture ..."

Photograph albums of the world there in his eyes, baby eyes, old man eyes, and all the dying eyes of the world.

"All right, so you may as well know the rest. If you can take pictures of someone's face a few second from now, you can take pictures of someone's face a few years from now ... same gimmick. Pick a cue, any cue. Always need a peg to hang it on. Remember it's all a matter of timing. Just time just time just time ... Come along, young man. Quite a few gimmicks to learn. Show you around the darkroom where the future develops. Quite a few gimmicks to learn. Reversed negatives and all that. Now some of these negatives you see here will develop tomorrow. Some have what you might call a long incubation period. Perhaps 'germination period' is more accurate. Seeds that grow. Well, you plant an acorn you know an oak tree will grow. So you planted it. Now other people can walk around over the spot where you planted the acorn and they don't know- ... Later on, when the film starts moving ... well .... see where I came in ..."

Flesh in an out of focus ... Vaudeville Jew with grey fish eyes ... 'Look, I nearly suffocated in gold letters ... there simply isn't room for any more from Las Palmas to David.' He looked through his sickness. Old friend flickered on screen, already old and brittle. Age flakes on a dusty sofa in sepia swirls, 'Don't know ... perhaps tomorrow ... ' Typhoid hints ... trying to break out of this numb Switzerland ... Casual adolescent came to the door ... age flakes fall thru a cloud of old photos ... voices frosted on the glass ... boys' thoughts and nurseries where English brainwaves raise a steady murmur ... Don't ask questions of receiving set, I really don't know ... Panama dust stirred words "I am dying, Meester? ... " Forgotten boy walked on screen and dusted off a magic smile ... Old financier flickered in camphor smell of cooking paregoric 'Don't know if you got my last hints from the Magic Lantern' ... Argentine ... Typhoid Epidemic in Switzerland ... old photographer trick ...

ages flakes fall *before* the shutter clicks . . . young boy thoughts long long ago . . . "I didn't know frequency waves . . . Oh yes I found out . . . the face dying just before I played the music and the subject never knew when . . . " Seconds clung to our bodies . . . cold coffee sitting right where you are sitting now with me . . . three in it now . . . on the sea wall . . . two of them tried to pay you . . . of course you got my last hints . . . Chinese characters you had to know . . . All right shifted commissions . . . you can take over my job now . . . silence all the photograph albums of old photographer tricks . . . all right, so you might as well know . . . it's all a matter of contact sparks . . . just time . . . just time . . . show you around the darkroom . . . quite a few gimmicks to learn . . . fossil negatives & all that . . . where I came in . . .

I take the last world there in his eyes. Timing. Just time just time out. Where the future develops. Just pick up the dark street. Age flakes a geometric arrangement of images reversed. Mirror images breaks out street riots. I was saying over and over: The picture awning flaps in your voice tomorrow's news.' Course we have Mexican picked out. Here's his album. Red & white striped T-shirt. Now let's step into the Magic Lantern. Sepia Park. Fountain. Trees. And me standing there superimposed over the park what looked like Chinese characters. Images reversed to that any image shifted the other. All right, old photographer's trick. Headline flashes on: Revolution in Cemetery. 'I am dying, Meester? In the darkroom?' It's helpless in Switzerland. Age flakes fall through the street. Muttering Greasy Jones so badly off, forgot his English. 'And don't remind me of frequency gauge . . receiving set exploded in that boy . . screen whisper anything . . Meester smiles through a ghost morning. So many actors and so little coffee. Death in Sweden or was it Switzerland? Three a week. Stayed all day. Charming. On the sea wall met a boy right where you are sitting now. All right, so take over my stale underwear. Under the ceiling fan personality reshapes, ages flakes in sepia, long long ago. I was saying over and over, reshapes where the awning flaps. Child forgotten coughing in 1920 street. What did they give you in 1920 Street? This lantern and that stale underwear, shirt flapping. You know that street boy in Puerto Assis. Empty. Stale summer. Speeding along the asphalt. Vines twisting through steel. Bare feet waiting for rain.

Smell of sickness in the room. Switzerland. Panama City. Machineguns in Baghdad. So many share old mirror. Trying to break out of this numb hotel. Pieces of finance on the evening wind. Tin shares in Buenos Aires. Mexican films muttering petulantly, old names waiting. Meester turned them out.

Young man came to the door. Some boy from vacant lot. Fading witness, still got officer bars. Child eyes look out across the nurseries. "Well it's all there in the files..." He pointed to stacks of old photos. "And here in the darkroom, waiting..." (death groans and screams rose in nitrous fumes) "... always plenty of that... and over here, youth... now that's a rare commodity and never enough to go around..." Boy voices drifted from the pictures. Young thoughts...

Your actors erased our remarks in long ago boy... the pilot eyes a dead world... 'Self no more is... I really finished... last cigar...' mutter of words in Ewyork Onolulu Aris Ome Oston... refuse of the earth... death takes over game... pieces of finance in mucus of the world... Switzerland summons no more... empty oil drums in Baghdad... last cold coffee waiting... so many actors buildings and stars laid flat for storage...

Remember I was film in Sweden... say goodbye, Johnny Yen's last adios... in and out of focus...

The Reporter found the hotel beyond a vacant lot by the old signal tower. HOTEL BELLEVUE in gold letters flaking off dusty glass. In the lobby sat an old Jew with grey fish eyes. The Jew waved his cigar. "I still got my cigar..." He put it back in his mouth with a subdued glint of gold teeth and looked out through the glass. A young man stepped forward flickering in and out of focus.

"What do you want?" he snapped. "The hotel is completely full. You understand, NO ROOM. None at all." His voice cracked like an old record. "Oh, but... you have come for the pictures... well, all right..." He led the way through dusty lobbies and corridors. Smell of resort hotels closed for the off season. Through living-rooms and nurseries a mutter of English governesses, 'Don't ask questions and don't pass remarks.' As they walked, the muttering voices followed and rose from old photos in sepia swirls that gathered around their feet.

The boy kicked petulantly.

"There's simply no room for you." He dusted off a magic lantern. "Now you see, with this lantern and that screen . . . it happens, you know, things can be done and so easily except so many things have happened and there simply isn't room any-more . . ."

Old financiers flickered in and out of his face. 'I own a piece of that boy . . . gilt-edged . . . but so many shareholders . . .'

The boy dodged sideways. "Oh shut up you silly old things! No I simply won't jack off in the outhouse . . . it's full of scor-pions for one thing . . . besides I'd sooner make fudge."

1910 watering places wind pieces of finance over the golf course summer afternoons drift in a sepia cloud . . . Do you see the silver fountains? words and music drifting from 1910 mus-taches twisting blue light in cisterns . . . Chinese characters walk words from the page . . growing out of the clay birthplace a passing transistor radio leading a child . . . junk sick from an old mirror Mr. Martin smiles . . . 1920s craps in the morning garden . . . hotel lobbies mutter the crystal tablets . . . through street crowds in Baghdad rising from the typewriter? I have passed by the urns fountains and figures . . .

Young witness in sorrowful servant down the clay steps . . . film gardens hotel lobbies muttering out of black Cadil-lacs . . Mr. Martin smiles . . . machinegunned in Baghdad . . . dark excrement on the urns . . . cold coffee wait-ing . . . all the old names coming down . . . old photographer trick waits by a vacant lot . . . cemetery flickering in and out of focus . . . a thin boy . . . Meester smiles . . . sepia clouds of Panama . . .

J. Brundage the newspaper man thanked the county clerk and apologized for taking up so much of his time. He walked out into the street swept by sudden shifts of weather so that at one minute the street was full of people walking around in shirt-sleeves, next thing they blew away in dead leaves. The old signal tower was covered with vines. He decided that nothing was gained by climbing it and started off on an angle until he was stopped by a high wooden fence. He skirted the fence until he found a loose slot and pushed through into a weed-grown vacant lot.

A large scorpion turned slow circles in the middle of a sand trap. 'This must be the old golf course,' he decided and dove into the second GPM. 'And come up in somebody else's septic tank sort of cool and clean, if it had been there ... some reward for 13 years of sweating converted cases ... what you might call a disputed clearing process ... so what with one thing and another deep into the third gulp which is just where the hotel is ... Arch's maps sort of leap out at you all at once ...'

THE INFERENTIAL KID

The Inferential Kid: a cool grey instance from Pluto so remotely disengaged that you can only infer his presence from that or this factor not quite in the same relation as it was before—when exactly? You can't quite remember. You add it all up, there is always something missing somewhere. A few seconds unaccounted for. A missing factor in any equation. The invisible mould of what is not that inexorably determines what is: The Inferential Kid from Pluto can blow up the planet with a pinhead or freak if you prefer, or as easily and coolly reorder the planet with silent shifts of his inferential departments or departures as the case may be.

Angle boys of the cosmos: haven't you forgotten someone or something? The name? Put down plain Mr. Jones, or just Mr. J. Occupation? Well, say tourist . . . I've been called harder names and it won't hurt my feelings . . . . Have you forgotten the deal that turned out a little better than you thought it would, and you thought maybe you were a little smarter than you thought you were? (if such a misconception were possible, and it is always, and it always was with such a stupid organism . . .) Or the deal that didn't turn out and you never could figure quite why and talked about 'gremlins in the darkroom' across the urinals of Present Time? Between the object and the photo? Between the conception and the act? Between X and Y falls the cold remote inferential shadow.

I *am* the Morphine that disappears in your canine preparations at Lexington. I *am* Apomorphine. What stood between the junkie and the pusher? Between the alcoholic and the cocktail lounge? What upset the film set of drunk-again-hooked-again? Angle boys of the cosmos: CAN you infer? I *am* the time unaccounted for between the camera and what the camera takes. I *am* the mark who wises up when he couldn't wise up. I *am* the power that beats the film studio with a box camera, a regiment of tanks with a defective slingshot.

Angle boys, small timers, with your operation this or that, your insatiable appetite for what is not yours and hope to make it yours, by lies and impudence, your fraudulent claims: the grey ash of Pluto blown from my sleeve ... dead cigarette ashes ... the unfinished cigarette ... Who is the coolest player? The player who is the farthest away from the game, the most disinterested in it. His limits are wider, and in consequence he can see further.

I must win in any solar system game because I am the factor in the system that is farthest out in the system, that is, in numerical terms. And what trumps any machine system factor is Saturn all the way OUT of the system game, gentlemen. Show your cards all players or get out of the game.

The Inferential Kid calls you all in the name of Hassan J. Sabbah or plain Mr. J. if you prefer. Calls you from the cold pinpoint of Pluto. Time is radioactive. It ticks away on the Geiger counter. There's very little time left. Show your cards all players.

The Blues live in remote cool offices under a steady silent rain of bank notes. Blue light on board meetings and mergers, and when any member leaves the board room the other members turn to each other slow and cool and say, "Errand boy ..." and nod out a thousand years on how cool they said it because the whole point of this game is to 'keep cool.'

"Remember what happened to Q.J.? Got the hot slide for his Mayan stinker ..."

"Errand boy ..."

So keep cool. The cooler you are here the longer you last. And above the Blue, remote cold strata of the Greys. Cold grey metal faces and pinpoint eyes shooting the heavy silent Plutonian ray blight whole planets at a glance.

"Kid, remember when you first got a bang of the Blue? That cool blue metal fix?"

"If god made anything better, he kept it for himself ... and he did ... and, Kid, it was the Grey ... talk about heavy metal kicks ... sure, I know you been cool ... but you never been really *cold,* baby, inside and out. Ever feel that liquid air in your spine and you move slow and heavy and hard to stop as a hydraulic jack? Ever shoot that metal ray out your pinpoint grey eyes? It don't shoot exactly, it just falls slow and heavy, you're that far up ..."

The Greys drifted in on a London particular, all in grey suits and grey overcoats and grey felt hats, pinpoint metal eyes spitting the silent deadly rain of Plutonium, reduced the earth to a cold slag heap, a grey cold ash. 'We like things quiet and cold. We *are* the Ultimate Weapon. We *are* death. When they call us in, any war is over.'

"Inasmuch as heavy metal is radioactive you will understand why keeping cool or better still: cold, is of such uh vital concern to the heavy metal factors. The actual charts that plot the E.T. (Explosion Time) of any unit are so complex that no machine can process them with any degree of accuracy as the cool credits keep sifting in. No doubt about it, Kid: the cooler you are the longer you last. And whatever you do, don't ever get involved with a Hot. Know what kind of people the Hots are? Well, I'll tell you. Now here is this young agent all decent and comfortable in his blue room listening to the junk note in his head like any nice average citizen when there is this goof in the machine the way it happens when folks get uncool and give too many orders going every which way and a whole block goes autonomous and the machine is downright honeycombed with these sabotaging separatist sons of a short circuit . . . so anyway, one of these awful bloomers dumped a rank hot writing to a clean-living heavy metal home this white-hot centipede on the floor just spitting out more heat from the fire head of a super nova. In vain our intrepid young agent said: 'You are uncool.' Well, he said it and he said it heavy and they went up together. You see when you bring a hot and a cold together, well uh . . . Now in this corner we have the old oven champ Sammy the Butcher. He is hot as a nova and sharp as the razor inside. And over here is the coldest Cold of them all, the Old Doctor from Pluto. Just hope they can drag it out until I get my bags backed . . ."

"Oh don't worry about all that junk, John. Can't you understand? Any second now the whole fucking shithouse goes up . . ."

"Now Mary you should have let me say that . . ."

"I tell you, John, there simply isn't time. Come as you are, John."

"Well now, Mary, let's not fly off the handle here. I'd like to sleep on this thing and have a talk with my banker in the morning..."

"Bows on stage, John...JOHN...*the doctor is on stage*...and you know what that means in showbiz..."

"Now Mary, don't panic...personally I have great faith in the apomorphine treatment, just tune out the old thermometer ...think of the saving in energy...why, it could all be channeled...so we got the Uranian cool blue junk and the Plutonian cold grey junk, why not Plutonian apomorphine...? Not for nothing will I be known as Nelly the Disconnector..."

"The mob won't stand for it, boss. They'll take the place apart..."

"What place?..."

His radioactive bones trailing the green guards and oven commandos remember he showed you the switch and put your hand on it...unfinished cigarette where the story ended. Now you can never thank him. He isn't there when he does you a favor. The only favor he can give is his silence his absence forever. Go on press the switch. You will notice it has no name and no symbol. It is attached to nothing. You will notice further that it is not a switch but the mould of a switch and cigarette smoke slowly fraying at the edges drifting up to high cool corners of the room. So little grey men of Pluto in their grey suits and grey felt hats played in his block house and went away through an old blue calendar.

Sitting in his cold grey metal office, the blind wizard ticks away as machines turn and white smoke of death spreads over a blighted planet.

"It is precisely then the continuation of organic life in its present form that can be regarded as our uh program? (...faulty...faulty...) However, we strongly suspect that any uh instance with uh such a seemingly uh insatiable appetite for organic life in any form can not be uh too far removed from what it eats. A man *is* what he eats...Old cannibal proverb. Borne out by the now classic experiment with planetarium worms in which our technicians conclusively established that any behavior which the experimentor could by any means at his disposal invoke (oh yes, we can pull a few switches...easy way & tough way thru any maze...) and the easy way worms come out with learned behavior patterns which are immediately assimilated by cannibal worms who eat the maze grade worms. These front office browned nose worms having been reduced by the experimentor to slices which the less venturesome worms could easily feed upon—and what better food than one's very own stock? keeps a worm fat happy and sluggish. So we cannot but feel that the uh sucking instance is uh motivated by somewhat more uh earthly considerations than a mere uh disinterested distaste for the smell of organic life . . . Where they come from there is no smell because there is no life to smell. They do not improve you. They have come to eat. Which brings us to the Clean Kid. Also known as Amplex Willy, also known as Mum Daisy. Now Daisy she is one lousy lay but she sure as hell is clean. One thing nobody can say is Daisy stinks. Because Daisy just doesn't smell at all. The Clean Kid doesn't smell and you won't smell either after he cleans you out. Yessir, when the Clean Kid walks on set everything just gets cleaner and cleaner until it is you might say completely CLEAN, and no smell to it at all. It's the only way to live clean, Kid. And that's what we always say up here in White Neighborhood is keep clean. Small-timers keep cool and keep cold, we just keep clean. And that way we win . . .

"You win exactly *what?* A place to be clean in? Why can't you just go off and be clean by yourself on some nice clean white planet like a tile bathroom in Stockholm? What's your need for the dirty folk if you is so white as clean as you smell?"

"Point is, Kid, all these factors no matter how cool cold inferential or downright clean they might come on have been weighed and found all too heavily in-terested . . . and time ticks away on the Geiger counter . . ."

"But I tell you, doctor, Plutonium *is* fissionable . . . *highly* fissionable . . . why, this could lead to . ."

"You uh exaggerate, Doctor Unruh. And uh frankly we don't like to hear the word 'fissionable' here . . . still less the word 'Nova' . . . these are dirty words, Doctor . . your job is research, pure clean motiveless research. So if uh our directives may at times seem uh misleading, please remember that it is uh better to ah exceed than fall short of the uh mark . . ."

The Doctor on stage and so it all ended. "Yes, you have been a very sick uh whatever, Mr. and Mrs. D, and all those things you

132

thought you wanted—power, junk, money, control . . . you didn't want them. Not really. Just look out the window: sunlight on an old wall. A very old wall. It was a long time ago and nothing here now. All the old Halloween masks are in a St. Louis ash pit. Dead smoke of an unfinished cigarette. Sure you said a lot of things you didn't mean. But that won't happen again. You see, I cancel all your words forever. You will never have to be sorry for what you say again. Because you won't say anything. No more is written. I do my work, pack my bag and go. Cross all your skies see my Rx: SILENCE."

LAST AWNING FLAPS ON THE PIER

The town is built on a shelf of gray shale around an inlet of the lake. A pier of rotting wood extends out into the shallow green water over bottomless ooze infested by a species of poisonous worm. There is one small island in the inlet on which grows a twisted swamp cypress. Beyond the inlet the green water extends out into a vast delta with pockets here and there of deep black water and finally the lake itself stretches to the sky. On the inland side the town is surrounded by hardwood forest. The town people depend for food on game from the forest and fish from the lake. Owing to the shallow water unnavigable for a craft drawing more than a few inches, their boats are light structures mounted on pontoons with large sails to catch the faint winds stirring in this area of terminal calm. The sails are made from old photos welded together with a strong transparent glue, the pictures creating a low pressure area to draw the winds of past time. They also fish from dirigibles under which are slung a boat shaped cabin, the fragile craft floating a few feet above the water propelled by pressure jets from a porcelain cylinder (there is no metal in this area). The houses are made from blocks of gray shale soft as soapstone, the entire town forming one hive like structure built around the inlet. The town people are without words and sit for hours on the pier and on balconies and terraces overlooking the inlet silent and immobile as lizards following with their eyes patterns traced in iridescent ooze by movements of the worm.

On closer inspection the houses are seen to be made from old photos compacted into blocks which give off a sepia haze pervading the rooms streets and terraces of this dead silent rubbish heap of past times—(a parenthesis stagnant as the green water and the postcard sky)—On the inland side of hardwood forests live hunters and subsistence farmers who sell their pictures to the town people in return for the procelain cylinders—Quote Greenbaum, early explorer.

Sad servant of the inland side shirt flapping trailing the smoke of hardwood forests offered us his pictures of a squirrel hunt—black rainwater and frogs in 1920 roads morning sleep of detour—luminous terraces moulded from old photos and leaves—silent grocer shops in cobblestone streets.

'Remember the needle beer at Sid's speakeasy?'

On the inland side a thin boy looked for me here on a St. Louis corner bits of silver paper in a wind across the park. Nothing here now shadow structure mounted on old newspapers of the world—(Caught a riot in Tangier from a passing transistor radio. Little winds stir papers on the city desk dirigibles through a violet sky rising from India ink)—Never the broken film opens for me again. Silence falls softly on my vigil from a black Cadillac.

'Remember the needle beer at Sid's speakeasy?'

Never the 1920 movie open to me again—smell of ashes in stone streets—his smile across the golf course—Last silent film stretches to the postcard sky. India ink shirt flapping down the lost streets a child sad as stagnant flowers.

'Remember I was abandoned long ago empty waiting on 1920 world in his eyes.'

Silence by 1920 ponds in vacant lots. Last awning flaps on the pier last man here now.

February 22, 1965
New York.

THE BAY OF PIGS

John turned slowly and noticed in the far corner of the bar room what he thought for a moment was a piece of statuary. A slight movement like breathing told him that the creature was alive. It was a girl with bright green eyes and the immobility of a lizard. He thought of a beautiful green reptile from remote crossroads of time.

The Southerner winked broadly. "Don't be shy, young man. Better go over and join her before some of those Mexican coyotes beat you to the jump ... She's been giving you the eyes for the last half hour."

The man turned and made his way through the crowded bar with extraordinary agility for a man of his bulk.

John picked up his drink and walked over to the corner. The girl looked at him steadily.

"Mind if I sit down?"

"Not at all," she said in a curiously unaccented English.

He sat down.

"What will you have to drink?"

"Creme de menthe, I think."

She gave him a look of cool appraisal from hooded green eyes deeply set in high cheek bones. Her eyes caught points of light in the room like an opal, and her jet black pupils converged and he had a feeling of being touched right at the source point inside his skull. The skin of her face was transparent, smooth, of a greenish pallor.

She sat absolutely immobile, looking at him. Slowly she smiled.

"The Bay of Pigs intends to make use of you," she said.

"You think he is CIA?"

"He's not trying to hide it ..."

"But what use could he make of me?"

"He is looking for the books of course."

"That story about the Mayan books being still in existence somewhere? You think there is any truth in it?"

"He thinks so, or he wouldn't waste time with you. That

means that others think so as well."

She looked around the room. A sprinkling of politicians with Chapultepec blondes, a table of loud Americans.

"Come, I will take you to a party ... It happens only once a year and you should see some of the real Mexico, something that will not last much longer ... folklore you might call it."

They walked out and turned right along the Paseo. Across the streets in the Alameda people strolled and talked and sat on benches. They walked down to the intersection and turned right again on Niño Perdido.

She was wearing flexible low-heeled shoes of green lizard skin that gripped the pavement as she glided along. He found it difficult to keep up with her.

It was a neighborhood of *pulquerias* sandwich booths and market stalls. Men in white cotton pants, in from the country. The sour smell of *pulque* and sweet urine was heavy in the air.

They were walking now on unpaved streets. They had reached a large dilapidated building, a black and empty warehouse, straight walls of masonry rose into the darkness.

She knocked at a heavy door with a little barred window. A man peeped out, opened the door and they walked into a corridor.

"*Buenas noches,*" said the doorman.

They walked down the corridor into a large room where a number of people were standing sitting laughing talking. Several of them greeted her and stared curiously at John.

Seated behind a desk in a dentist's chair was a massive woman like an Aztec earth goddess. She stretched out a hand to the girl, "*Buenas noches,* Iguana," she said. She turned her hard black eyes on John.

"*Buenas noches,* Gringito. *Bienvenido a la casa de Lola la Chata.*"

She took his hand in a powerful grip, her eyes with pinpoint pupils heavy and cold on his face and body.

The girl took his arm. "Let's get a drink."

He looked around.

There were bottles of tequila on a table, washtubs full of beer bottles on ice. On a long table beside Lola's desk he saw a number of syringes in glasses of alcohol. Men would come in and shake hands with Lola and she would reach into between her massive breasts and pull out a little packet and give it to them. Then they proceeded to the syringe table for a shot, nonchalantly administered in full view of the guests.

Mariachi singers were singing ranchero songs and several couples were dancing.

The addicts sat in chairs with hooded eyes like drowsy lizards. Sharp reek of marihuana drifted through the room.

Suddenly John saw several uniformed police.

"Police!" he cried. "It's a raid!"

The Iguana laughed. "They have come for their uh little present..."

He saw that the police went to Lola's desk and after shaking hands she opened a drawer and handed each policeman an envelope. The police were drinking beer and joking with the guests. One of them puffed on a marihuana cigarette letting the smoke out slowly through his mustache.

"Quite a party," he said.

"Yes, it's once a year on her birthday that Lola la Chata gives this party and on that day everything is free. On that day she gives. On other days she takes."

She took his arm. "Come, it will be noisy here."

She led the way through a back door upstairs and through a maze of corridors and empty rooms with the windows boarded up. Finally she took out a key and opened a door.

The room was small but well furnished with rugs and low tables and a large bed.

"Take off your shoes," she told him.

She sat down crosslegged on the bed and indicated that he was to sit opposite her.

Once again he felt the strange touch inside his skull that made him feel at once excited and uncomfortable as if he were a small boy naked before his gym instructor.

"Have you taken LSD?" she asked.

"Yes. I didn't like it. That metallic taste in the mouth."

She nodded. "LSD lets you out into a bad area. The plants are better. And they must be prepared in a certain way."

She got up and walked over to a corner of the room. He saw jars on shelves filled with herbs and dried mushrooms, and a table with earthenware pots and a spirit stove.

"I will now prepare for you the sacred mushrooms according to the ancient formula."

She lit the spirit stove and placed a pot of water on to boil, selecting pinches of herbs and dried mushroom, adding a little more, crooning over the mixture, an odd little tune.

He lost track of time. Perhaps it was the marihuana cigarette he had smoked at the party. There was a sudden hiatus, it seemed ten minutes but it must have been much longer.

"The mushrooms are ready," she said and handed him a little gourd of liquid.

He drank it down.

She poured one for herself and drank it.

They sat down on the bed.

Almost at once he felt a rush of dizziness that was not at all unpleasant, in fact it was he decided very pleasant indeed.

Now the walls and rugs were twisting in strange shapes, and then suddenly sensuality hit him in a wave, his flesh was writhing, dissolving in green fire. He wanted to tear off his clothes. His lips swelled with blood and blood sang in his ears.

He looked at her helplessly.

"Stand up," she told him.

"I uh..."

"Stand up."

He obeyed and stood there in front of her, his pants bulging.

With cool precise fingers she unbuttoned his shirt and slipped it off.

She unhooked his belt, opened his pants and with a quick movement slid his pants and shorts down. He stood there blushing as the blood rushed to his crotch and his penis began to stir and stiffen.

She stood there and watched. Suddenly he remembered an incident of his early adolescence. He had been barely fourteen at the time. A gym instructor had visited the house. His parents were away. It was after dinner and the man was looking at him and he felt something uncomfortable. Then the man said, 'I'd like to see you stripped.' He said, alright, his mouth was dry and his heart was pounding as he led the way to his room, Oh god, he thought, suppose it happens? He tried to think of something else. Then he was in the room, the man sitting down on the bed, he took off his shoes and socks and shirt. 'Come over here,' the man said. He stood in front of the man who ran his hands over his arms and shoulders. He was feeling very relieved that he didn't have to take down his pants. And then the man was undoing his belt and pants and suddenly his pants and shorts dropped and he was standing there naked blushing furiously, and it was happening, he couldn't stop it. The man looked down. He glanced down and bit his lip and a little whimper burst from him. The man said, 'Your little pecker is getting hard.' And then, knowing it was alright he felt a rush of excitement feeling the man's hand on his buttocks and thighs, it was all the way up now pulsing throbbing, and he didn't care. Then the man sat him down beside him on the bed, and as he sat down a drop of lubricant squeezed out. At that time he had never masturbated. Then the man's hand was on his nuts and penis. 'You've been playing with this?' He leaned back on his elbow, legs stretched out. 'Well . . . yes . . . a little bit . . . ' 'Did you ever play with it until it went off?' 'No. How long do you have to play with it before that happens?' The man's hand was rubbing the lubricant around the tip of his penis. It happened in a few seconds and he was spurting hot gobs up onto his stomach. Afterwards, the man left town and he had put the incident out of his mind. Now standing there naked the memory came back and the excitement.

And suddenly he had a curious feeling that perhaps she wasn't a girl, and a feeling too that there was somebody else in the room.

She was slowly stripping and when she stood naked her body was almost inhumanly beautiful, the smooth green flesh and the obvious strength of her breast like green fruit. She pulled him down onto the bed and suddenly they were rolling in an ecstasy of lust.

He felt penetrated and penetrating the soft gelatin between her legs that pulled him in further and further, they twisted from one end of the bed to the other, she was on top, on her side, silver light popped in his eyes and his head seemed to fly to pieces. He glimpsed a sky rocket bursting in someone's head, in his brain. The Van Allen Belt.

When he got back to the hotel the landlady told him that his friend had arrived. As he walked up the stairs his heart was pounding with excitement feeling the ache and stiffness in his groin.

He opened the door.

She got up off the bed laying down a book and walked to the middle of the room to meet him. She was dressed in men's clothes, khaki pants and shirt, jodhpurs, a green tie.

He threw his arms around her kissed her on the lips . . .

Suddenly a shock went through him. The chest was hard, he could feel the ribs. This was a man's body.

He shoved the other back. "Why, you're . . . !"

"I am the Iguana's twin brother."

John stood there blushing furiously, his pants sticking out straight at the fly.

"Why be embarrassed? After all, I was there . . ."

He remembered the presence of another person in the room, and the feeling that it was alright like the time with the gym instructor. His embarrassment turned to lust. Why not? They were in tune, how could it matter?

"Let's have a look at you," the boy said. He reached out with his long cool fingers with precise movements performed at unbelievable speed. He unhooked John's belt unbuttoned his pants.

Before he fully realized what was happening his pants and shorts fell to his ankles and he stood there his shirt moving slightly in a wind through the open window.

The boy looked at him and licked his lips with a little red tongue. His black eyes shone with an inner light. He walked around John touching his buttocks and genitals with fingers that left a cool burn like menthol. He brought a chair and placed it behind John who sat down.

The boy slipped off his soft boots; shirt, pants, and shorts followed, and he was standing there naked while John was still fumbling with his shoelaces.

The boy knelt at his feet, quickly removed John's shoes and socks, pulled his pants and shorts off and hung them on a wooden peg.

John stood up and took off his shirt.

The boy was thinner than his sister, he had the same smooth green skin, his penis erect throbbing was a pink purple color, the

141

pubic hairs jet black and shiny.

Then the boy was kissing him, running his tongue inside John's mouth. A musty odor came off his body.

The boy led him to the bed. He was rubbing an unguent on John's penis that left a cold burn. John felt suddenly strong and confident, he shoved the boy on his back, pulled a pillow under him and pushed his legs up. The rectum was the same purple brown color as the boy's penis. John rubbed some vaseline on and slowly shoved it in, feeling the rectum pull him in with a soft muscular pressure. As he moved in and out feeling the gathering tightness in his groin, John was suddenly holding the girl, feeling her breast against him and then the boy again, feeling the hot gobs hit his chest.

They quivered together a few seconds. They lay there looking at the ceiling.

"I had to make it with you, you understand."

John did not understand.

"Let's get dressed. I want to give you some idea as to what is going on here."

After they were dressed, the boy began: "We know a good deal about your background, otherwise I wouldn't be telling you this. For example, we know about the gym instructor."

John looked at him in amazement. "How could you know that?"

"There are ways to find these things out. Ways which you will learn and learn quickly if you are to be of use to us. The story about the books being still in existence is true. That is why the Bay of Pigs is here. And others as well . . . Russians, Chinese, Swiss . . . *very* clever, the Swiss . . . In consequence, Mayan scholars are now at a premium."

He got a briefcase and took out three packages tied with a ribbon.

"Copies of the Dresden, Madrid and Paris codices. You have seen them of course."

John nodded.

"Now look here." He pointed to a priest who was making an incision in what looked like a man plant. "What do you make of it?"

"Nothing much. They worshipped a corn god. No doubt this is

142

some mythological representation."

"It is a representation of something quite definite. It is a flesh tree."

"A flesh tree...?"

"Yes. What we call flesh is in point of fact a vegetable. It literally grows on trees, or rather it did."

"But that's fantastic!"

"The agents of five countries don't think so. You have already had a visit from the police, have you not?"

"Yes... they were looking for drugs."

"They were looking for any pretext to get you out of Mexico. They take orders from B.O.P., The Bay of Pigs."

"But why? After all, they need Mayan scholars..."

"They already have the best. Besides, I don't think you would care to work for them when you learn what they are doing or what they intend to do... They intend to keep the books secret. Top secret. Classified. To monopolize the knowledge contained in these books."

"But how could they do that if it is as important as you say?"

"Quite easily. Don't be mislead into thinking it is just rivalry, to be the first to claim an important discovery."

"Just how do you and your sister fit into this? And what do you want from me?"

"We.represent.the.Academy."

John was about to ask what this was when he noticed a change in the boy's face. The face blurred out and a middle-aged man was sitting there, sharp birdlike face, cool imperturbable grey eyes.

"The original statement of the Academy as simply an institution or series of institutions where knowledge skills and techniques methods of training, physical and spiritual, Scientology, Karate, Aikido were coordinated and taught is simply a strategical move to drive the enemy into the open with nothing to declare but their bad intentions. Here it is possible in terms of present day techniques. Why isn't it being done? Why is all knowledge and skills kept from the youth of the world? These questions were aided by the Academy program. Since then of course we have gone underground to prepare for all-out resistance. We select and train our personnel in a number of locations.

You have been selected for training. You ask, who is the enemy we are preparing to resist. There are several basic formulas that have held this planet in ignorance and slavery. The first is the concept of a nation or country. Draw a line around a piece of land and call it a country. That means police, customs, barriers, armies and trouble with other stone-age tribes on the other side of the line. The concept of a country must be eliminated. Countries are an extension from another formula, the formula of the family. Parents are allowed to bring up helpless children in any form of nonsense they have themselves been infected with. The family in turn derives from the whole unsanitary system of reproduction in operation here. It is now possible to create living beings. Not bacteria and viruses in a test tube, but human or at least humanoid beings who have not been crippled by the traumas of birth and death. The two beings who brought you here are preliminary experiments. The womb is now obsolete. The enemy is those beings and forces who have devised and enforced these basic formulas, and now threatened by the loss of their human slaves will do anything to keep these formulas in operation.

The secret of flesh is in the lost Mayan books. All the forces of suppression have now converged on Mexico to find these books and keep this secret from being used to create a new race of beings on this planet."

FILE TICKER TAPE

Tuesday July 7 (St. Aubierge) 1964 Tangier

Tuesday was the last day for Singing Years. St. Aubierge (ambiguous sign of an inn) ... Last day for signing years ... (ambiguous sign of an inn) ... St. Auberge or St. Lodge if you prefer sounded the Sts. on

a trumpet. Stand in for Mr. who?? My name was called like this before ... rioters bleed without return. *We want to hear pay talk dad and we want to hear pay talk now.* Yes that's me still there wait

ing in the empty Tangier Sts ... sunshine and shadow of Mexico ... A night in Madrid ... You let this happen?? (holding the laser gun in his hands) ... wrecked market half buried in sand ... smell of blood and

excrement in the Tangier streets. ("We won't be needing you after Friday returning herewith Title Insurance Policy No. 17497") You don't remember me? Showing you the papers I carry ... diseased bent

over burnt out inside ... coordinates grangrene ... *Hiroshima* gangrene/"Frankly doctor we don't like to hear the word nova here." Bringing you the Voice of America: "This is November 18, 1963. This is

Independence Day in Morocco. The Independence is in the harbor of Tangier. The Independence is an *American* boat. The *American* Independence is in Morocco. This is Independence Day in Morocco. This

is *American* Independence Day in Morocco. This is *July 4th* 1964 in Morocco!"/Brook's Park ... the old swimming pool kinda run down now. Mack the Knife over the loudspeaker. I can feel it where the

old tonsils used to be ... ether vertigo. (He has loosed the fatal lightning of his terrible swift sword). 'Somebody goofed. The patient is hemorrhaging ... clamps nurse ... quick before I lose my

patient.' (He has sounded forth the trumpet that shall never

145

call retreat). *Ghostly looking child burned a hole in the blanket*
... brief flight to Gib. Our business now has no future. Know human

limitations?? Captain Clark welcomes you aboard. Set your watches and clocks back sixty-five units. Five units unaccounted for. Remember the show price? (Holding the gun in his hands) You

don't remember this sad stranger there on the sea wall wishing you luck from dying lips terrible bright sun exploded between us? And remember the "Priest" ... They called him and he stayed ... (Boat

whistling in the harbor ... Well that's about the closest way I know to tell you and papers rustling across city desks ... fresh southerly winds a long time ago ... going through the files like this

Captain Clark welcomes you aboard ... agony to breathe in sad muttering voices: "How is this for an angle, B.J.? Now the boys back of Barry Goldwater are pretty smart boys ... ('Now Barry he's a shade slow but then he don't have far to go') ... and the way they figure the board is this: Evoke provoke prod con pay if you have to but catch those Niggers gone coon out in *open armed revolt against the United States of America.* So then we declare a natural emergency and take over. So then we teach those queers and dirty writers dope fiend degenerates to act like decent Americans. So far it's cut and dried, B.J.... peg to hang it on. Hitler hung it on the Sheenies we hang it on the Shines but maybe we don't *stop* there so watch yourself Jew boy. Remember we like *nice* Jews nice Jews with Jew jokes. Sax Rohmered the whole script in *President Fu Manchu Consul Edition* ... Now how is this for the old reverseroo. B.J., are you listening? ... So the Niggers is playing it Martin Luther cool down the bus line and the Black Muslims just practicing away at their judo like good 'uns called their boys off the street ... Well it don't look good to Barry and the boys. So the boys resort to desperate expedient ... (just how desperate they had no way of knowing at the time) ... They called in a writing Nigger to organize and write a revolution with a promise of bleaching him right out after. After the Nigger saluted smartly and left the board room B.J. turned to N.D. and said slowly and nasty: We going to bleach that guy out?"

And N.D. said slower and nastier: "Sure ... He wants his ass white ... We'll burn it white ..."

But the Nigger is a double agent see? A.E.? Sure he will write a revolution but he is out to *win* with Chinese help and Moscow gold you understand. So the *revolt* breaks out yes you guessed it right in Barry's home state of Arizona if my memory serves ... town of Nogales on the border and it isn't *happening* the way Barry and the boys had it pegged in the Deep South spreading to the Northern cities ... Action ... Camera ... rape ... murder ... atrocities ... public outcry ... the Strong Leader. Yeah we got him under wraps. (too bad about Barry). But it isn't happening like that. It is happening like *that:* highly trained *guerrilla* units and demolition teams hitting all communication centers ... hit and move ... When troops move in they dodge over the border ... The boys follow ... Mexico protests. The raids continue ... We shell a border town ... (Dead boy there in the dusty street). Rapid deterioration of the relationship between the two countries ... America invades ... China sends troops ... United States' forces occupy Mexico ... the occupying *forces face a solid wall of hostility* ... snipers ... sabotage ... blank cold Indian faces ... from the Rio Grande to the Argentine the guerrilla forces operate, trained and led by *Chinese.* Chinese overrun Southeast Asia. We are holding Formosa at heavy cost. Russia, armed and waiting. The American High Command complained they could not get their hands free to throw an atom bomb. "It would land right on our back porch," said the Secretary of Defense yesterday before a Senate Committee investigating what they termed "criminal diffidence in the use of atomic weapons." Widespread power cuts have immobilized the deep freeze. Armed bands prowl the Northern cities ... ("Where you going with all that food Gertie? Home to mother?" They have stopped a fag on North Clark St. You can see his heart fluttering like a bird under the blue silk shirt under the cold eyes and searching guns ...) Beatnik saints preach peace look love ... "I mean just wrap your ass around a neighbor and love him all over into one big family of gooking come and contented assholes." China invades Canada. Or we could slant the whole script another way casting Lodge as the Rube on a *Real American Stand.* "Everything America ever stood for in any man's dream America stands for now. Everything this country could have been and wasn't it will be now. Every promise America ever made, America will redeem now ..."

Agony to breathe in *The Boy's Magazine* ... As I have told you sad guards remote posts ... Came to a street half buried in sand ... transitory halting place in this mutilated phantom ... smell of strange parks ... shabby quarters of a forgotten city under a silent steady rain his cold distant umbrella to the harbor office. The Captain's Log Book Feb. 5, 1899: "It was a long time in such pain used address I give you ... "

Last intersection there ... smell of ashes ... tin can flash flare ... Wind stirs a lock of hair ... hock shop kid like mother used to make ... A distant hand lifted sad as his voice: "quiet now ... I go" ... flickering silver smile ...

Now we could slant the whole script another way B.J. The American way. Now the Fascist conspirators have arranged the assassination of Goldwater on TV so they can unwrap the Strong Leader and break out White Con 17. But this confused assassin, this Puerto Rican Red Jew Chinese Nigger, his senses fuddled by injections of Marijuana, blasts Scranton instead of Barry ... "You can imagine how I felt" he exclaimed later at police headquarters ... Public outcry led by Mary McCarthy ... A Trotskyite Jew in Yonkers married to a Nigger girl writes a book called *The Fascist Conspiracy.*" While you wait Mary McCarthy and Norman Mailer organize a Militant Writer's Union. All American writers recalled to base ... stand by for orders ... Yes that means you Paul Bowles. All you jokers in the Shakespeare squadron return to base immediately and stand by for orders.

The Frisco Kid he never returns. In life used address I give you. Going to reach Frisco? "Agony to breathe in this mutilated phantom ... last interesection the dim jerky faraway voice." Old junky selling Christmas seals on North Clark St. ... the "Priest" they called him ... used to be me? Mister?? ... used address I give you.

It's the greatest story conference in history B.J. All these writers assembled in a warehouse of The Atlantic Tea Co. ... (move out of the way for rats) ... These writers are going to *write history as it happens in present time.* And I don't want to hear any Banshee wails from you skypilots. Now the way I figure it is this: America stands for *doing the job*. Take that assassin back there blasting the wrong man. Now I remember when killers were artisans and took pride in their work. That's what's wrong with America today . . . half-assed assassins . . . half-assed writers . . . half-assed plumbers . . . a million actors . . . one corny part. So we write a darn good part for every actor on the American set. You gotta se the whole scene as a show. Now you take those rural lawmen down in Cunt Lick County. "Just happened to be out slopping my hawgs when the boys burned that old Nigger. They shouldn't have done it like that" . . . old hoofers . . . Clem and Jody . . . the Kids from the show . . . Report to Actors' Equity.

Remember show price? Know who I am? "Field of Grasshoppers" is my name. "Olive tree North of the bushes" is my name. "Goodbye Mister" is my name . . . Wind and dust is my name . . . Never happened is my /

Remember show price? Know who I am? Yes talking to *you Doctor* D. and *you Board* members. I don't talk often and I don't talk long. You didn't

want to pay the Piper. you didn't want to talk apomorphine— (note)—You shut the door on the Nova Police. Too late now. The Piper is over the hills

and far away. Merk has stopped making apomorphine. Inspector Lee is on vacation. You smell Hiroshima? You see this laser gun looking right through you?

You know who I am now? Señor Deadline has come to call. Keep your Great Amber Clutch on the table, Doc. Did you think you could call me and not pay

you welching amber as in yellow Board bastards? Set your geiger counters forward an hour. Captain Clark welcomes you, A Board. Last rights. Mr. Deadline

is *here* to call

THE MOVING TIMES

February 10, 1964.

"We will Travel not only in Space But In Time as Well."

A Russian scientist said that. Let's start traveling. Form the words into columns and march them off the page. Start with newspapers like this: Take today's paper. Fill up three columns with selections. Now read *cross* columns. Fill a column on another page with cross column readings. Now fill in the remaining columns with selections from yesterday's papers and so on back. Each time you do this there will be less of present time on the page. The page is 'forgetting' present time as you move back in time through word columns. Now to move forward in time. Try writing tomorrow's news today. Fill three columns with your future time guesses. Read cross column. Fill one column on another page with your cross column readings. Fill the other columns with tomorrow's newspaper. Notice that there are many hints of the so-called future in your cross column readings. When you read words in columns you are reading the future, that is you are reading on subliminal level; other columns on the page that you will later experience consciously you have already read.

January 17, 1947

English made easy for Beginners. It revolves flexible formula.

For beginners today we are going to study the verb *fix*. I fix I fixed I have fixed. The general meaning of *fix* is to fit together or put in place as I fixed the notice to the board. Another meaning is to arrange: I fixed the meeting for four o'clock. Still another meaning is to set right or put in order: I fixed that up all right. Or it can mean to put somebody in his place; I will fix him once and for all. Other meanings are to fix a date to make a date for more advanced students suffering is one very long moment, we cannot divide it by seasons. We can only record its moods and chronicle (1) their return. With us time itself does not progress. It revolves. It seems to circle round one center of pain. The paralysing immobility (2) of a life every circumstance of which is regulated after an unchangeable pattern (3) so that we eat drink lie down and pray according to the inflexible (4) laws of an iron (5) formula (6) extract from *The Depths* by Oscar Wilde (1) Chronicle to record in writing, (2) Immobility fixity (3) pattern design (4) inflexible implacable (5) formu-

September 17, 1899

Last Gun Post Erased In A Small Town Newspaper September 17, 1899.

'Mr Bradley Mr Martin' stood there in dead stars heavy with his dusty answer drew September 17, 1899 over New York that morning giving you my toy soldiers put away steps trailing a lonely dining room cool remote Sunday. Stein's army has sailed for South Africa fresh southerly winds a long time ago for such a purpose. On assigning them to duty the books opened. Last Tuesday was the regular day for signing years. A committee lad born and bred again refused the contract or even had the opportunity to do so. They are all valueless as I know from my blind wait between London and Brighton a distant hand couldn't reach never came out that afternoon at recess time I watched the torn sky bend with the wind white white white as far as the eye can see a blinding flash of white. The cabin reeks of exploded star. It was a long time ago young man you can still see used to be your brother young cop whistling 'Annie Laurie' if my memory serves on the top floor you can watch our worn out film dim jerky far away shut a bureau drawer. Last gun post erased in a small town new-

a should again arrive from
ome by train as they did in
re war days in four days'
ime the romantic broadcast
n the history of radio after
enturies of silence I will
ix him once and for all to
date another meaning is to
rrange a meeting for 4 cross-
olumn readings A Russian
cientist said for beginners
oday 'Mr Bradley Mr Martin'
aid that let's start there
n dead stars from the word
nto verb *fix*. I fix I fixed
heavy with his dusty colu-
ins have fixed the general
nswer drew September off the
age. Start with meaning of
x is to fit 17 1899 over
ew York newspapers like this
ut in place giving you to-
ay's paper. Fill as I fixed
ie notice to my toy soldiers
ut away up three columns wi-
 the board. Another meaning
:eps trailing a lone *cross*
 to arrange: I fixed room
ool remote columns. Fill a
lumn on the meeting for four
clock Sunday. Stein's army
as another page with still a-
other meaning is to set right
 put in order the remaining
lumns or it can mean a pur-
ose on assigning papers to
ut somebody in his duty books
 back. Each time place I fix
m on opened. There will be
ss for all. Advanced stu-
nts refused the contract
oved back in time through
ffering. WE cannot do so.
:y writing tomorrow's mood
rward in time and my blind
ait between news today colu-
n seems to circle that after-
on in recess on another pa-

ge with you one center of
pain I watched the sky torn
column sky bend with the wind
after blinding flash of light
the cab in reeks of exploded
star can still see used to be
you you are completely deserted you can still see the old
fence there by the creek silver ghost boy of exploded star dim jerky far away sad muttering voices. Come closer.
Listen: Las whispered 'Good
bye, Mister. "Cool remote Sunday last report you are reading the future on (5) formulae (6) to record in writing
our worn out film dim jerky
far away. You will see days
run backwards again in four
days like the train did. distant hand couldn't time guesses to the last broadcast.
"You don't remember me,
Mister?"
 You will see 'me' tomor-
row and tomorrow and tomorrow
to the last syllable of recorded time because you have
written and read 'me' today.
You still don't remember? Your
memory of the future will improve in columns. Now try this: take a walk a ride do some dreary errands in these
foreign suburbs here sad voices dirtier older worn out film shut away in a bureau drawer drink a cup of coffee maybe read the papers sometimes
TV in the Cafe de Paris. Baby,
it's *foreign* outside has the
general meaning of alien and
or hostile. So return to your
trap by taxi and *write* what
you have just seen heard over-
heard read felt with particular attention to intersection

points like 'You come with me,
Meester? Moulin Rouge. Good
place. Spanish boy girls no
cost much'/or an English lesson on television in the Cafe
de Paris sad toy Place de France. 'It's a long way to Ti-
pperary it's a long way to go.'
"This is the fourth lesson 1
2 3 4. There are lessons on
television. There are many
lessons on television. This
is the fourth lesson. See what I mean? Intersection points and few of them are good
however you can form your old
plays into columns and move
back in *your* time using the
same method you will by now
have applied to newspapers. Or
you can write your dreary walk before you take it. Until
you find the only walk is out.
Now what have I done here in
these columns? Well the first
column is my necessary expla-
nations. The second column is
from the *Tangier Gazette* Jan.
17, 1974. The third column is
composed from texts of my own
interspersed with pieces from
the *New York Times* September
17, 1899.

Pages from the
Cut-Up Scrapbooks

The following pages, copied from the fragile artifacts themselves, are choice selections from the famous notebooks which for decades William S. Burroughs toted with him through deserts, dead roads, and cities of the night, creating (with the sometime collaboration of Brion Gysin) a paste-up conglutination of Moroccan streets, weird news items, St. Louis memorabilia, ruminations on sex and death, old photographs, notes from narcs, and other essential exotica—an incredible montage of telescoped existence on the main line, source material and matrix of his books.

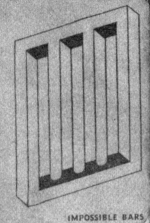

IMPOSSIBLE BARS

Met "Nadam..
meure in a
bar, introduced
him to alan
Curren and
others. a shark
had been butch-
ed and
pieces of the
meat were
laying about

damp cold   the cold spring news
rooms flashing flatter   on a top floor
                    nobody there

LLOYD   ○○○○○◖

We have been inspecting your
air shuts an   empty and
many years   afternoon Mr.
il ne suffit   Muter?
were   J.C.   room 18   me
heureux. L'ouvertu   Simon   with
land est originale et sp   fart
rités curieuses. Et c'   le   that
et le même chef qui   les feuilles
la première fois en E   mortes? play
alto de Bela Bartok, 1   lie. trust you?
William Primrose, o
puissan
conce   Première rehearsa   our neighbors
giggle and   ter la répétition
whisper some   tres.   **LE MONDE.**
thing   due   E
room with rose   coal stain
wall paper   go
run out across   you
the river   was
an evil river

pour alto
tonie de Carl
é un véritable
l'ennui,
ombre d'œuvres
différents pro-
était moins
e contempo-
positeurs de
plus gu

nchons le
sées l
en second
numéros qui
qu'au cirque
fait que l'on
levard Roche
le? Les clé
opoème gi
sur un

JANVIER

8 MERCREDI. S. Lucien   8-358

(Associated Press Wirefotos)

Omaha television announcer John F. Johnson (left) was indentified by John and Richard Bader, of Akron, Ohio, as their brother, Lawrence Joseph Bader (right), who disappeared on fishing trip in 1957. Johnson denies kinship.

I can feel the heat closing lake that
day and he was presumed in army special to the new drowned after his
motor boat the St.Foriegnor was found
beached and empty at Ohio ticker
rumors.Take a picture.That's the
point a drunk policeman.Brother Law
jumped out on them 8 years ago.Nobody
knew the dead policeman and he is
missing **brother** applied for that
station.It is the same man from the
TV beyond prints were taken in Chi.

What is	this	evil	thing	J.S.???????		4
broken	glass all	over the	floor in			5
the bathroom.The		Countess	steps			
up for	the French	sytem	of identif			6
		ication				7

      ⚛ Mod. N° 26-104 ⚛

1	2	3	4

I can see the empty bench in the
distance there by the lake far
away the price blured in smoke and
whirlpool's of the fumbling West.
a violet fog over the city..
 !Mort,I'm coming'

THE EMPTY BENCH

HERE THE YOU COP WAS SITTING.

He dropped the photo into a bureau drawer smell of ashes rising from the typewriter a black silver sky of broken film. Wasn't anything to say. 'Mr. Bradly Mr. Martin stood there on dead stars heavy with his dusty answer drew 'September 17, 1899' over New York he waves his hands sadly turns them out: "Giving you my toy soldiers put away steps trailing down a windy street exploded star between us. last resort. Come closer. Listen. Station ends the last smell of blood and excrement whispered on a fence, 'Goodbye, Mister.'

toys put away soldier's goodbye on a windy street half buried in sand. Dead stars splash his cheek bone with silver ash.

Fresh southerly winds a long time ago over New York shirt flapping with the torn sky a distant hand lifted. "Good bye, Mister. Used to be the man you're looking for. Couldn't reach. Breath never called opportunity to do so." 'September 17, 1899, cool remote Sunday' distant 1920 wind and dust: "I have opened the gates for you." He waves his hand sadly from the lake from the hill from the sky. Remember the boy's room

The British Journal of Addiction | Vol. 53, No. 2

Doctor J.Dent: 'Apomorphine is a
metabolic regulator'.

... ON JANUARY 11 TWO DAYS ... IN APRIL 355
will be successful.

January 1957

I met D.K. at the R.R.station
'Walk in on people and claim
to be God..that ridiculous waltz
faster faster..I've got to get
out there' and he rushes for a
train after serious rioting brok
broke out May §Square Panama Jan
II and I am muttering §never
thought of myself be anything
but an explorer dangerous area
making an explorers decisions
He is running down the platform
I find my train 23 for Alaska
come North out of his body
what mouldy genital pawn ticket
sad as his voice cracked 'know
who I am?'

..Take a woman's dull
ominous prerecorded advice..blind
voices on the phone..(allen G)
Russ Fawcett? Yes he's still there
asleep now'..' I rcognize your
arty way of asking for me' 'We
have not seen each other in a
long time' (Ian has lost a leg.
When he sees me at the table he
leaves without speaking.Russ
follows.Might be just what I am
look prerecorded warning in a
woman's voice..artificial arms and
legs..soulless winded words..'
'smoking orgy packett..Ian..
 Columbia I8..sputtering blue
ponchos..Accident in which you
St.Hill, lost your sight.Well
coldest Lexington.I have the
unhappy mountain road in earmuffs
blind voices on the phone.'

Red umbr-
ella in
he tapi
Rooks at
the air port
nihon -
t api soma
us connu
met Board
jimmy the
guide -
to meet you?
he'ant want
him "He
at Gallimard
of Norris?
in the office
umbrella
same red
saw the
Later &

Yet Claude
Gallimard
looked in
a closet.
Avon nova
Cosmetics
The tapi
locked in
Rook's closet
avon nova
nihon Cos-
metics. Our
barman is
fucking up
Ashley Hotel
Restaurant
open to.
non resid-
ents. Queen's
Mews, until
eye

Mc Carter
theatre at
long last
Jazz buffs
Cool it with
the Modern
Jazz Quartet
8:30. Save
hundreds of
dollars.

Today we are going to
study the verb fix.
layout to the map and
Still another meaning is
Departed have left
er or put in place, as
won't be there long.

general
meanings is   I fixed
the notion
to the Board

m. L.

Not knowing where to start . . .

1937 over Princes Square

18   Feb I8,I95? ice   18,248

out of Paris,

the future   blured and buckled

word in his throat that were not his.

"Somewhere Hayseed.

over the Rainbow?

· homesweethome scene:

· · ·"prolonged excessive use", . .

getting so little

typewriter" time see you I   HOI

retain some

· affection for home town scars.

Sunday, September 17, 1899

On The Back Porch Of His Farm

Martin, Bradly Martin, Mr. Bradly Mr. Martin sat down on the back porch of his farm. He slipped a bag of Bull Durham out of his shirt pocket with two fingers and started rolling a cigarette. He paused listening. He finished rolling the cigarette, put it between his lips and went back inside, lifted his gunbelt off a peg and hung it on. He lit the cigarette and sat down on the steps waiting.

Five horsemen stopped just outside the gate. They sat there looking at him and not saying anything.

"Why tell me, Arch?" said the dead leaves and there was a blue shirt and cigarette smoke

"That's mighty close, Clem. Funny I didn't see you."

"You had your back turned."

"Well it isn't turned now, Clem."

Martin just stood there after that not saying anything and there wasn't anything to say— just cigarette smoke drifting in the still afternoon and Martin's pinpoint metal eyes looking through the smoke. Arch turned his horse abruptly. The party rode away. Martin went back and sat down on the porch

Sunday, September 17, 1899

On The Back Porch Of His Farm

H. William

The beginning
is also the
End. And

who is
the third
who walk
beside you
the begin-
ing w
is a
a th
begin

the be-
ginning
who is
also the
third

is Wednesday th[e]
beside you be
begin   is also
third wh[o] 3Rd
                who is
                who is
while a drum came by
beating of a strange
manner of beats now
and then a single stroke
which my wife and I
wondered at what the
meaning of it should be

begin
who is
also
walk
out you
the third
who is
beside
you ??

JUIN

9 MARDI. Ste Pélagie

1956

Blood in   Sarah who returned
sputum in   the laugh a cop
morning   [A.W.] who last
returned   is a cop in Baghdad
last night in Baghdad from Hiroshima
from Hiroshima   one is laser guns
noticed that tempted on the table
is refused to use in the
chocolates for pressure Tangier
Breakfast   um bom Café

La Policía ha procedido a la de-
tención de un tipo de cuidado que
llevaba una extraordinaria carrera
de estafas en Tánger. Abdeselam
Ben Ahmed Merabet, alias «Chocolate», de 23 años, estaba prepa-
rándose para casarse y quería dis-
poner de un equipo completo para
que no faltara de nada en su nuevo
hogar. Y gracias a un sistema que
le dio excelentes resultados llegó

his XXXXXXX   Vietnam
father at the   behind
diner table It   lines
is a North Af   ed by
rican city.   long
Casa? Algiers?   with tile
Cairo? With   was on
Martin in an   hole in
other room.   and a
Blue light.A   openings
garden outside get out with self hid
what looks   Martin.Hotel   boy abou
like a giant   arranged for   plained
spider but is   the space   involvin
some one with   travel party   y towels
a cloth mask   Some one intr r than
over his mou-   rduces me to   cock hid
th and nose.   biting the
The mask has   bed on Price   consular
caught fire.   Road some int Rosset
Woke up back   visible thing was
in Price Road. plucked at the
soap.Martin   covers.I coul **to**
Hotel Old   d see now the
Bank by Ros   walls were br **make**
set.Yes he   ick. Ginger
arranged for   walked out th
helicopter   e door.The
the conquered   room was movi
   ng.Stops now
                and I can see
                red sign in **carpe**
the window.I   rabic outside

Old Arch
OTES DE SEPTEMBRE *These our actors,*

ter the Big Survey.   *standing there with the cold spring news*

e last carnival is
eing pulled down,
uildings and

THE COLDSPRING NEWS

```
Annie Lauri
never call
ed retreat
Mister this
is mile end
```

stars****

t *in Tangier?*

aid flat for storage

```
orth Clark St
Priest cabled
```

In these foreign suburbs here, I fixed *the notice to The Board.*

/Sunday   *the* Red Witch *went sky high."*

:alling Woolworth/ *Sky full of holes*
'The Red Witch' went
sky high/8 Crystal.

```
S. Theodore Maynan/
Losing along (Inter-
```

```
I looked at
the dogs and
I looked at
the pavement
Stand in fo
Mr. WHO
```

```
September 17, 1899.
```

```
Last Gun Post Erased In
A Small Town Newspaper
September 17, 1899.
'Mr Bradley Mr Martin'
stood there in dead star
-s heavy with his dusty
answer drew September
17, 1899 over New York
```

"The Man Who Never Was."

Quién es?"

Day Martin's Book Store
opened if my memory serves
did'nt use those photos
lose his blood opposite
Woolworth's there are
lessons on television
"Que tal# Henrique?"
Your very own prose get
small prize washed back
on Spain repeat perform-
ance page he managed to
wrecked markets streets
covered by black silver
dust of broken film sun
sling and shadow of Madrid
Hem managed to shove the
door open walked out into
the streets of Madrid..

22
23
2
3
12
13
14
15
16
17
18

```
                 a cavern
                 a boiling
                 cauldron
12   IUDenter the   2   317-49
                 3 witches
                 (Put the
                 'Cauldron'  4
                 on 'Hill's
                 Own' with   5
                 Luther in
                 space****   6
                 Harper      7
```

Sensing that Harper is on casual
work-('By The Great Black Rock
 of Karsim he can hear my thoughts...gobble gobble) cool and
casual hotel room in London....

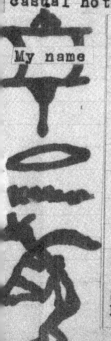

```
                 cries:T'is
                 time t'is   8
My name          time curse  9
                 go back
                 curse go    10
                  back back
                 with double 11
                 fear and
                 flak double 12
                 double toil 13
                 and trouble
                 fire burn   14
                 and cauldron
                 bubble
                 towers open 16
                 fire--take
                 towers in   17
                 Spanish
                 Hill 32     18
                             19
```

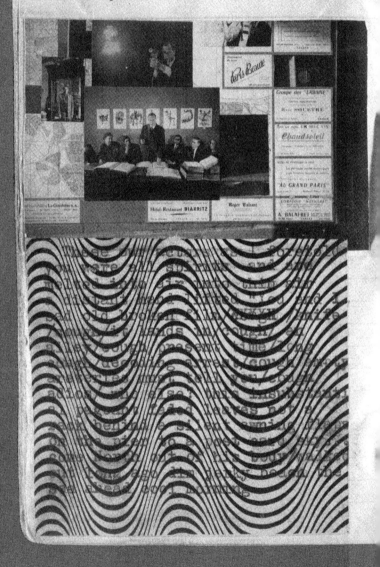

damps things down and they
stay the same underneath
he would say in his slow
serious way.A product from
a St.Louis chemical comp
any called Apo 33 a synth
esis of the apo-morphine
formulae described as a
metabolic regulator in-
dicated for anxiety intox
ications and addictions..
apo-morphine does its work
and goes. Synthesis of the
apo-morphine formulae could
create drugs excercising a
regulating instance ten or a
hundred times more powerful
than the existing formulae
drugs capable of eradicating
from the planet what we now
call anxiety. Now since most
existing establishments are
basically and immovably rooted
in this same anxiety it is not
surprising that the use of the
apomorphine treatment and the
development of synthetic
variations of the apomorphine
formulae has been and will
continue to be violently
opposed in certain interested
and drearily predictable
quarters of the Western World.

On closer inspection the houses are
seen to be made from old photos
compacted into blocks which give
off a sepia haze pervading the
rooms streets and terraces of this
dead silent rubbish heap of past
 times,--(a parenthesis stagnant as
the green water and the post card
sky)--On the inland side of hard
wood XXXXXX forests live hunters
and subsistence farmers who sell
their pictures to the town people
 in return for the porcelain
cylinders--Quote Greenbaum,early
 XXXXXX explorer

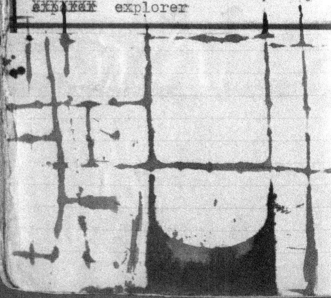

JALIDU AVE . ST LOUIS .

IRS. MURPHY'S ROOMING HOUSE

DECEMBRE

20 DIMANCHE. S. Théophile 355-11

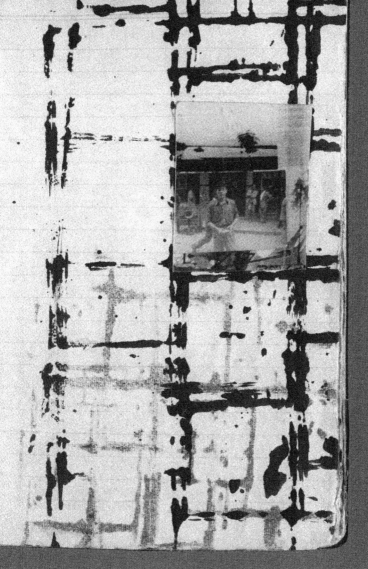

all God's children got time

41

44

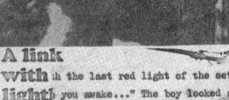

A link with lighth

...h the last red light of the setting ... you awake..." The boy looked at

... in with the last red rays of the

FOR most just names blazed like a comet and dimed out
radio's shipp
Fastnet, Ske.k and the rigging and circling guls.
- but they're
lathered rock chill of interstellar space. He
house keep boy's face was covered with a white
them, situat
of the world .inted in his ruffled hair. John
coastline.

Not so k the cabin..."
crews by bo.... could be delayed by weather for as
much as four to six weeks.
Not any more, thanks to two
English helicopter pilots,
38-year-old Captain Frank
Laycock from Hertfordshire
and 32-year-old Paul
Midgley from Oxford.

These men work for Irish
Helicopters out of Dublin
and Shannon and, with their

turbulent air conditions, on
handkerchief-sized concrete
patches hundreds of feet
above the waves or on
stilt-supported pads set
into the precarious rocks.

Conditions can be so ex-
posed that in strong winds

Said Captain Laycoc
after landing on Gre
Blasket Island: 'There's a
immense appeal about he
copter flying. You have
much greater illusion
freedom in flight than in
fixed-wing plane.

Captain Laycock with his Alouette III jet-powered helicopte

na his whole body shaking John
ng the bones like a starved cat
ut the bandana in his coat pocket
h blood smiling as he licked the
e setting sunu as the shadow fell
nally on the circling gulls. The
to be white with a crust of
ys hair. A chill settled over John's
o have been standing there for hours

The abandoned brigantine Mary Celeste was 'fit to go round the world'

The Retreat Diaries

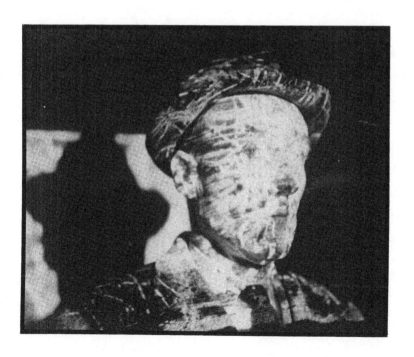

THE RETREAT DIARIES

INTRODUCTION

When, after riding with William Burroughs slowly out over Vermont hills on the back of a wooden trailer to the little hut where he would be in retreat for two weeks, I stood with him in front and said goodbye, he turned his head to the slip of grass twirling in his fingers, almost shyly—as though a little embarrassed he should be seen about to go in to himself for a time. When I returned from New York two weeks later, he stepped out of the hut in bright sunlight, grinning and maneuvering a walking stick cut from a hickory branch. He surely had travels to tell, and yet the five-hour ride back to the City was mostly silent, as together we concentrated on the darkening highway and our own thoughts.

Soon after he was re-established in his working routine, I asked if I might look at the dream-notes he had kept in his red day-book. In a few days I had transcribed them and shown him the new manuscript, which he eventually used as a starting point for an essay on the retreat itself and the associational framework of the dreams recorded. After the essay was completed and we had conceived this book, Burroughs asked me to include a dream of mine which was the source of one of his dream characters. Also included is a dream of Allen Ginsberg's from 1960, in which he visits the Tibet of his imagination and there confirms that Burroughs is secretly a Buddhist agent.

This essay, I think, is a major statement of the dilemma any artist faces if he begins to take Buddhism seriously. In Burroughs' case this dilemma was all the more explicit for that his invitation to the retreat was specifically qualified by a request that he not bring a typewriter. He had balked, in a furnished room in Boulder last summer, asking his host Chogyam Trungpa Rinpoche what he should do then if a literarily useful idea came to him on retreat. But when Rinpoche compared Burroughs' typewriter to the carpenter's saw and the chef's utensils, he saw Rinpoche's point and agreed to comply. The idea, of course, was that quiet self-examination and meditation removed from the means of compulsive self-expression were more important to him than any writing he might produce. I believe that Burroughs gave this idea a fair trial.

—James Grauerholz

THE RETREAT DIARIES

Last summer in Boulder I was talking to Chogyam Trungpa Rinpoche about doing a retreat at his Vermont center. I asked about taking along a typewriter. He objected that this would defeat the whole purpose of a retreat, like a carpenter takes along his tools—and I see we have a very different purpose in mind. That he could make the carpenter comparison shows where the difference lies: the difference being, with all due respect for the trade of Jesus Christ, that a carpenter can always carpenter, while a writer has to take it when it comes and a glimpse once lost may never come again, like Coleridge's Kubla Khan. Writers don't write, they read and transcribe. They are only allowed to access to the books at certain arbitrary times. They have to make the most of these occasions. Furthermore I am more concerned with writing than I am with any sort of enlightenment, which is often an ever-retreating mirage like the fully analyzed or fully liberated person. I use meditation to get material for writing. I am not concerned with some abstract nirvana. It is exactly the visions and fireworks that are useful for me, exactly what all the masters tell us we should pay as little attention to as possible. Telepathy, journeys out of the body—these manifestations, according to Trungpa, are mere distractions. Exactly. Distraction: fun, like hang-gliding or surf-boarding or skin diving. So why not have fun? I sense an underlying dogma here to which I am not willing to submit.

The purposes of a Boddhisattva and an artist are different and perhaps not reconcilable. *Show me a good Buddhist novelist.* When Huxley got Buddhism, he stopped writing novels and wrote Buddhist tracts. Meditation, astral travel, telepathy, are all means to an end for the novelist. I even got copy out of scientology. It's a question of emphasis. Any writer who does not consider his writing the most important thing he does, who does not consider writing his only salvation, I—"I trust him little in the commerce of the soul." As the French say: *pas serieux.*

I was willing to concede the typewriter, but I certainly would not concede pen and paper. A good percentage of my characters and sets come from dreams, and if you don't write a dream, in many cases, you forget it. The actual brain trace of dream memory differs from that of waking memory. I have frequently had the experience of waking from a dream, going over it a number of times, and then forgetting it completely. So during the retreat I kept pen and paper by my bed, and lit a candle and wrote my dreams down when they occurred. As it happens, I got a new episode for the book I am currently writing and solved a problem of structure in a dream recorded in these diaries. I also attempted some journeys out of the body to visit specific people, with results that, while not conclusive (they rarely are), were at least interesting and fruitful. In short, I feel that I get further out through writing than I would through any meditation system. And so far as any system goes, I prefer the open-ended, dangerous and unpredictable universe of Don Juan to the closed, predictable karma universe of the Buddhists.* Indeed, existence *is* the cause of suffering, and suffering may be good copy. Don Juan says he is an impeccable warrior and not a master; anyone who is looking for a master should look elsewhere. *I am not looking for a master;* I am looking for the *books*. In dreams I sometimes find the books where it is written and I may bring back a few phrases that unwind like a scroll. Then I write as fast as I can type, because I am reading, not writing.

I will endeavor to summarize the highly complex and sophisticated system of spiritual training outlined by Don Juan in *Tales of Power*. The aim of this training is to produce an impeccable warrior—that is, a being who is at all times completely in possession of himself. The warrior is concerned only with expressing the totality of himself, not with praise or support from others. He neither seeks nor admits a master. The warrior's state is achieved with the aid of a teacher and a benefactor. To understand the respective roles of teacher and benefactor, one must consider the concepts of the *tonal* and the *nagual,* which are basic to the warrior's path. The *tonal* is the sum of any individual's perceptions and knowledge, everything he can talk about and explain, including his own physical being. The *nagual* is everything outside the *tonal:* the inexplicable, the unpredictable, the unknown. The *nagual* is everything that cannot be talked about or explained, but only witnessed. The sudden irruption of the *nagual* into the *tonal* can be lethal unless the student is carefully prepared. The teacher's role is to clean up and strengthen the *tonal,* so that the student is able to deal with the *nagual* which the benefactor will then demonstrate. The teacher and the benefactor show the student how to reach the unknown, but they cannot predict what will happen when he does reach the *nagual.* The *nagual* is by its nature unpredictable, and the whole training is extremely dangerous. While the *tonal,* the totality of conscious existence, shapes the individual being, the *tonal* is in turn shaped by the *nagual,* by everything it is not, which surrounds it like a mold. The *tonal* tends to shut out and deny the *nagual,* which takes over completely in the moment of death. If we see the *nagual* as the unknown, the unpredictable and unexplainable, the role of the artist is to make contact with the *nagual* and bring a part of it back into the *tonal* in paint or words, sculpture, film, or music. The *nagual* is also the area of so-called psychic phenomena which the Buddhists consider as distractions from the way of enlightenment. Buddhism and the teachings of Don Juan are simply not directed towards the same goals. Don Juan does not offer any final solution or enlightenment. Neither does the artist.

During the retreat I wrote down dreams and the elaboration of dreams that takes place spontaneously in the waking state. I used an exercise in association: take a walk and later write down what you were thinking when a deer crossed the road or whey you sat down on a rock and killed a biting fly. One of my first acts in my retreat hut was to improvise a fly swatter from an old whisk broom, and I think this no-killing obsession is nonsense. Where do you draw the line? Mosquitoes? Biting flies? Lice? Venemous insects? I'd rather kill a brown recluse spider than get bitten by one. And I will not coexist with flies.* Interesting point here: The Miracle of the Centipede which disappeared as I was about to kill it with a sledge hammer. That was a nice miracle. *Chapeau,* Trungpa Rinpoche. Because that centipede was only half an inch long, and they don't get much bigger in that climate. And that's a bearable size—doesn't keep me awake knowing it is in the room, so why kill it? On the other hand, a centipede three inches long is already an abomination in my eyes. Little spider in web at window. He's all right. But I hear a rustling on the shelf above my bed. I light the candle and there is a spider about an inch across and a brown spider at that. Might be a brown recluse. Any case, too big to live in my vicinity. I feel better after it is dead, knowing it can't get on my face while I am sleeping.

The Retreat Diaries are not a sequential presentation. By sequential presentation, I mean Monday with all dreams and occurrences noted, then on to Tuesday and so forth. Here Thursday and Friday may be cut in with Monday, or the elaboration of a dream cut in with the dream itself in a grid of past present and future. Like the last words of Dutch Schultz. Some of Dutch's associations cannot be traced or even guessed at. Others quite clearly derive from the known events of his life. The *structure* is that a man is *seeing a film* composed of past present and future, dream and fantasy, a film which the reader cannot see directly but only infer through the words. This is the structure of these diaries.

To start with dream August 9th, 1975 . . . "WORDS" Perhaps women *are* words, and as Brion Gysin says, the first words were "Hello." When God anesthetized Adam and made Eve out of his rib and he comes around, Eve says "Hello Adam." Recall when Pat Garrett had surrounded a cabin where Billy the Kid, Charlie Browder and a few others were holed up. Charlie had just stepped outside to piss and caught a .30-.30 through his guts which knocked him back into the cabin and Billy shoved him out with a gun in his hand. "Try and kill one of them before you die." Charlie starts staggering towards Garrett, pissing in his pants, spitting blood, dead on his feet without strength to lift the gun, so Garrett holds his fire. He gets right in front of Garrett and says "I wish . . . I wish . . ." and collapses hugging Garrett's knees and Garrett says quietly "Hello Charlie."

Death is a word. Now fairy stone was an old remedy for sunburn, and they say it's hot on the planet Venus. Words can also serve as cover. Words are a painkiller, like junk. And here is dream about Doctor Dent, who cured me of the junk habit with apo-morphine treatment.

The Diaries consist of bits of dreams and poetry and associations cut in together; I can't cover every association, jut give a few examples. I was thinking about Bradbury Robinson, an English friend who was then going in for mystical Christianity, when a deer crossed the road. Spanish subtitle on the film *Rashomon*. The woodcutter had deceived the police and stolen a ring. And some spaced-out Buddhist has put the fire extinguisher *under* the Coleman stove. I can see burning fluid falling in a sheet of flame while somebody tries to reach the extinguisher. Move the extinguisher to a better place.

Now to contact Campbell Dalglish by the method outlined in Monroe's *Journeys Out of the Body*. His instructions are to visit a place and not a person. That is, you concentrate on where the person is. Now Campbell lives in a house outside Conifer, Colorado and he works in Denver. So in the dream I am on Wyoming Street and find I am in the wrong house, since my house is on *Denver* Street. Someone else I tried to contact some days later was John D.C., who was later—much later—at Little America in Wyoming and sent me a postcard. Point is, this out-of-body visiting is not a sequential matter. There is no time outside the body, or rather, past present and future merge. So don't expect a simple one-to-one visit; it doesn't always work that way. On August 7th I set out to contact my son Bill in Santa Cruz, California. Dream about Madrid. Now years ago in Tangier I had dream that I was standing with Bill on the coast and saw an explosion in the distance, and said, "There goes Madrid." Also, Santa Cruz is a Spanish name, and California used to be Spanish. And a sort of fast-moving agent story emerged from this dream.

Contact James Grauerholz. Lumbago helped by his back exercises. Contact came later and indirectly. James had related a dream to me about a fundamentalist sect and meeting a young boy who said, "Shall we camel?" (The dream is quoted in an appendix.) This boy then slots into this dream via a friend named Camel, and this is the episode which showed me how the pirate story I was working on could fit into *Cities of the Red Night,* at precisely the point where the excerpt published in *ARCADE* is in the manuscript. And it was James who selected that excerpt, and sent it in to *ARCADE* during the retreat.

Someone has written on a piece of cardboard in the woodshed: "How can I please myself when I have no self to please?" Sorry, young man, I think you are kidding yourself. As long as you talk to yourself, you have a self. The self is like a pimping blackmailing chauffeur who gets you from here to there on word lines.

"Maya am I? You don't get rid of me that easy."

I have always felt that the essence of self is *words*, the internal dialogue. Trungpa agreed, with reservations, but does not give the matter of words such basic importance as I do. Don Juan, on the other hand, says that suspending the internal dialogue is the crucial step out of a preconceived idea of self. *Tales of Power,* p. 22: "To change our idea of the world is the crux of sorcery. And stopping the internal dialogue is the only way to accomplish it." The exercise he recommends to stop the internal dialogue is to walk with the eyes slightly crossed, covering a 180-degree area, without focusing on anything.* This floods out the internal dialogue. Unfortunately I had not read *Tales of Power* at the time of my retreat and have had no opportunity to perform this exercise. It is not really practical in a city, owing to the constant barrage of word and image.

Some years ago I put a question to CONTROL, a mysterious computer in London which purports to be from Venus and will answer any question.

Question: Would rubbing out the word result in immediate exteriorization from the body?

Answer: Yes.

Question: How can this be accomplished?

Answer: At first automatic exercise.

I took this to mean that once the words talk on their own, they rub themselves out.

As a writer I deal with words. The more characters and sets develop on their own, the more valid they are for artistic purposes. If I was reading and not writing, I would literally be out of my body and into my sets and characters, like a painter who bowed three times and disappeared into his painting.

A basic mutation in consciousness is necessary. No patchwork will do the job. Nobody sitting in his body is egoless. What is the nature of this drastic step into the unknown? As Korzybski said, "I don't know. Let's see." This is the Space Age. Space is a dangerous and unmapped area. It is necessary to travel. It is not necessary to live.

Saturday, August 9th, 1975
Terrible quarrel with Joan, who wouldn't let me alone to go to toilet. I scream, "I hate you." She is rubbing something on me like green fairy stone.
"Words"
A young boy doused with gasoline and burned to death.
I was in England? An 80 year old woman asked me for methadone in front of 2 addicts. I slapped her face. "You could have the police here tomorrow"

Sunday, August 10th, 1975
Doctor Dent was in next room at the Empress. I met him in the corridor and went into the room which he shared with another man. The man told me "Doctor Dent is broke."
I had moved into room in the Empress with Ian. I have missed dinner. Dr. Alexander, a tall thin man in his 30's, trying to persuade me to do a reading in a small town. His Indian guide is there in a sort of sled. Two little men come in and do a juggling act.

Monday, August 11th, 1975
First day of retreat. Review the process. Beckett asked me to fish in his pond. Kiki has arranged interview with *Playboy*. In station with Ray M. waiting for train to St. Louis. Little house in New Orleans. In wrong house on Wyoming St., I live on Denver St. Material witness to murder in Spain. Have they caught the murders. "Yes" a cop says. "I have him at home. You see I used to run a discotheque." Ra Ra Ra Boomderay. I hurry to my blue heaven. Dinner with Bill Willis and Brion at Italian place. Best steak in town at Lucky Nick Dickendorf's. Roman ruins in England. Rented shack on river from D. Camel. Tandem toilet. "Shall we camel?" A toilet in Hell. Fight with the club steward. "I know what your game is." That damned bus. John Brady in New York with Pat. Blank inhuman look. Boy's Town on Price Road. Bradbury Robinson—deer crosses road. *Enganado a la*

195

policia. Rashomon. It would be good to hear from you. This heath this calm this quiet scene. Why kill snakes? This is Independence Day in Morocco. Ian will be in Paris tomorrow. Part soiled rope. Milk Weed Minnesota. I wear my trousers rolled. Karma is a word. There goes Madrid. The trolley in Alexandria. "Delodge where are the keys?" Dingy station yellow lights. The hour that darkens and grows always later.

Tuesday, August 12th, 1975

Long process in different forms. Infiltrating some branch of the Process. Alan Watson had brought presents from America. Ian there.

Wednesday, August 13th, 1975

Samuel Beckett sent letter asking me to fish in his backyard pond. And to accompany him on deep sea diving trip. He would need help.

An Arab beggar at table in Paris. I offered him a sugar lattice pastry which he refused. I said "Va'ton" (Beat it)

Boeing crash in snow covered mountains; cinders?

1. Dropped shaving brush which bounced into shrine by sea shell.

2. About to kill a centipede with hammer, by Trungpa's shrine. *Centipede disappeared.* By the sun: 11:45 A.M. Later saw centipede behind rock sheets.

Things needed. Shaving mirror. Anyone used to shave feels deterioration if he cannot. Mirror also essential in case of something in eye. Flyswatter. Fire extinguisher under Coleman stove behind trash bucket. If stove catches fire, dangerous access. Moved by wood stove. Condensed milk. Powered milk worse than no milk.

I twice missed path in walk through woods to find flowers for green bottle.

Thursday, August 14th, 1975

Chaos and gun fights. Confused alarms of struggle and flight. Shot cop. Where ignorant armies clash by night.

Kiki had arranged an interview with *Playboy.* I arrive on horseback. Army saddle. Playboy of the Western World, guitar is I love you. Words are made from breath. Your breath. Words need you. You do not need words. Breath from maid are words. Words are what is not. Knot is what are words. Words knot are what is? What knot words? *Our* is? What knot is? Our words? What words knot our is? *What?* Nor our words? Is? What is knot our words? Our words is not what?

Saw deer 12 noon by sun. Is word reverse mirror image of what is not? Try Chinese and Egyptian hieroglyphics in mirrors. Saw Ian as imp with red hair and pointed ears.

(To Friday, April 4th:)

The *Evening News,* August 14th, 1975. China blue half moon in the late afternoon sky. Note for G. Ferguson attached to milkweed. La Cuerda with a gob of mud from tractor. (8.2.7.6 on toilet paper) Sit. Bradbury. The deer. Left hand path around mud puddle. Walked to wall. She dwelt among the untrodden ways but oh the difference to me. Back to sit. Control needs time. Control needs beings with limited time who experience time. And few could know when Lucy ceased to be. Fair as a star when only one is shining in the sky. A violet hidden by a mossy stone, half hidden from the eye. Turn left. Sit. Sun going. LSD story. Mort. Day is done. Gone the sun. From the lake from the hill from the sky. All is well soldier brave, God is nigh. Back over pine needles. Twirling his club down cobblestone streets the sky goes out against his back.

Friday, August 15th, 1975

(To contact Brion, 10 P.M.)

In R.R. station with Ray M. and others. I was waiting for train to St. Louis. Meet me in St. Louis Louie, meet me at the fair. Ray had a whole room full of trunks and parcels. Later trying to find out when St. Louis train leaves. No Information. I was going to find out one way or another. Crowd barrier (Plan 28 at a quick glance) I had my ticket. Old steam trains. Dingy station yellow lights. Tickets. When is the next train for St. Louis?

Not much point in one drink.

(To Tuesday, June 3rd:)

St. Ian. St. Jacques. St. Allen.

Ian turning cartwheels in the dale. Ian in Paris today? Where is my little knife? When did I use it last? Can't remember. Let legs guide you toward the dip. Now I remember, to perforate cardboard note for G. Ferguson (wonder where he is?) Yes there it is by the milkweed. Got milk on hands yesterday putting up note. Harbor Beach, little gold knife. Part the soiled rope. Sit. Milk Weed Minnesota. Biggest milkweed and smallest people. Out to dale. Back. How many types of ignorance? The path. I am hungry. Back to hut. I wear my trousers rolled. Do I dare to eat a peach? Are they ripe yet? No.

Saturday, August 16th, 1975
   (To contact Campbell Dalglish)
   Went to meet Tim Leary in a restaurant in R.R. station off corridor. People there offered me food and vodka. Outside in corridor as I was leaving met Tim, looking quite different—long horsy face, brown teeth, like an English professor.
   I had a little house in New Orleans by the river. Coming home on my bicycle of light. Ah there it is: orange settee on front porch. Up driveway. Bicycle on back porch. Very small backyard plot behind for sale. Perhaps whole area to be taken over for levee? House was just two facades, front porch and back porch. Sled on back porch. I suddenly realize this is not my house, getting dressed on time to button shirt. Forget socks. Onto bicycle and open door in front drive. Down driveway as young man in tan knitted tie and light suit carrying suitcase crosses front yard. He calls to me "Delodge where are the keys?" I ride on, noticing that this is Wyoming St. and I live on *Denver Street.*
   (To Monday, June 16th:)
   House in dream half inside and half outside. Door to drive. Chairs. Front door opens on platform. Bed on back porch opens on backyard.
   Songs in head today, August 16th. Love Thy Neighbor. Ra Ra Ra Boomderay. For a nickel or a dime.
   Put aside spoiled peach for the raccoon. Last night he rejected an aubergine. I don't blame him.
   Word is another voice. Put your little foot right in. When evening is nigh I hurry to my blue heaven.

Sunday, August 17th, 1975

(To contact Bill Jr.—a mild gray day, Terre Haute 23)

Murder in Spain. The police... saw banner headline:

FRANCO DEAD

In Spain with some tourists in car. A bandit killed one tourist, cutting throat. Police arrived. We are roughly taken to Madrid police station. I say "Wait a minute. We are the victims, not the criminals..."

"Estan testigos," they say. *"Esperan aqui."*

I look around at the police. Two *agentes* discuss the way to *vigilar* a district for subversives. I see that they have modeled themselves on the Gestapo. A sloppy Gestapo in fact. One *agente* has a sort of alarm bell and leaps up to hit a suspect every thirty seconds.

Finally I am called to give my statement. By now they are more polite, realizing that we are people of some consequence. A lieutenant in the Identification Dept. receives me politely, shaking hands: "Lieutenant Rodriguez de Cocuera."

He types statement and takes picture, informs me that my luggage and passport will be returned and I am free to go after a visit to the American Embassy and an intimate visit to the Marquisa de Dentura. This woman is remote relation of mine by marriage. I have never seen her and have no reason to visit her or to think she would welcome a visit from me. However he makes it clear that this visit is condition of my release.

(To Wednesday, June 4th:)

Visit to Marquisa who gives me letter to be delivered in London. Subsequently the Lieutenant takes over the entire department and rises to rank of major and finally demands all the files of his rival Major Linares, head of the secret police.

To be remembered that California was Spain at one time. Dream years ago; I was with Billy in Tangiers. Explosion to the north and I said "There goes Madrid"

Clear demonstration that we do not control words: sub-vocal songs. As I shaved and straightened up this morning, "Just My Bill" from *Showboat.*

Lieutenant de Cocuera: Smallish, thin, clean-shaven. Heavy beard, blue-gray face, gray eyes. Deceptively mild, deprecatory manner as if to say of police beating prisoners in next room,

"*Those* apes." Very purposeful. Cool player. Tie-up with former Nazi in Interpol. Looking beyond Franco. Cool ironic glance at picture on wall: "They come and go ..."

(To Sunday, April 6th:)

Leaving police station I was treated with great politeness by detectives who had been brusque and suspicious before. One, a fattish blond man with pimples and cold gray eyes, shook hands. I asked if the murderer had been caught.

"Oh yes" said a thin plainclothesman in a gray suit, shoulders narrower than hips. "I have him at home. You see I used to run a discotheque."

A uniformed cop carried my luggage and called a cab. I checked into the Hotel Inglés, and took cab to address on card. The Marquisa, a middle-aged blonde with heavy makeup, received me, extending both hands.

"Ah the American cousin."

I accepted a tea. She looked at me over the rim of her cup.

"And now I have a favor to ask—a letter to be delivered in London. In person ... "

I didn't like it. The servant announced "The Count and Countess de Grazia."

"Oh what a bore. Those Yugoslavian Royalists. Why don't they just run a pig farm like their king."

The Count was a tiny man with a waxed mustache, obsequiously polite; the Countess buck-toothed and degenerate looking. When told that I had had trouble with the police, the Count was devastated as the Countess whistled through her teeth like an agitated chipmunk.

"Ah but you must go," said the Marquisa. "Your plane leaves in an hour."

"But I have no reservation ..."

"A reservation has been made."

"But my luggage ..."

"In the car outside." She embraced me and slipped a letter into my inside coat pocket.

Car: young officer, driver. Through customs to London. Christopher Brentwood, 6 Princes Place. The discotheque letter:

"Permissions on discotheque delayed as usual. I agree that this could be a profitable investment with proper management and selective clientele. It is to be kept in mind that we suffer from a time lag here, so selection of records must reflect the modes of three to five years ago. Regret that I cannot intervene directly, owing to my position, but I have not been remiss behind the scenes. *Wenn nicht von vorn, den von hintern herum.* (When not by the front way, then around by the back way.)

Sincerely Recorded,
Rodriguez de Cocuera

Suggest The Blue Ribbon as name for discotheque.

I read the letter and handed it back. "Mister Brentwood. I am not an agent on the political level."

"Neither are we. That is, not entirely..."

"Aren't you? Police officials? Former Nazis in Interpol... rich American Marquisas... No doubt the Lieutenant intends to get all the files in his department, including the coveted files of Major Linares, head of the secret police..."

Monday, August 18th, 1975
(To contact James G.)
Vague dream. Stage act with John D.C. Lumbago helped by James' back exercise. Was able to gather bowl of blackberries.

Tuesday, August 19th, 1975
(To contact John D.C. and Steven Low)
Checking out food at cafeteria counter. Clover-shaped pan full of milk. Hid quarter ounce of C in pocket.

Dinner plans in St. Louis involving Brion, Bill Willis, Italian place. Bill wanted a steak. I asked him "Where is best steak in town?" He said "At Lucky Nick Dickendorf's"

Still crippled. Put out sign. Will arrange to go to chiropractor tomorrow—Dr. Billings?

Wednesday, August 20th, 1975
John D.C.—Cities of the Red Night—A Roman temple in England on iron ore site—reference to poppers.

Sitting on couch. Light wouldn't turn on. Moved to another couch. "No no no."

Went to chiropractor Dr. Behrens, 19 Grove St: "I see all walks of life. Man was here complaining about 'the bus.' I asked him 'Are you a bus driver?' Turned out he was president of the Chase Manhattan bank. But he had to park his car every day and take a bus."

Broke kerosene lamp putting on FETISH T-shirt. Raccoon came to hut for tuna and rice. Watching him eat destroyed spider's web. The Spider's House.

Thursday, August 21st, 1975

With Paul Bowles and Ian. Showed them how I could fly. Tried to teach Ian who was wearing heavy grey lumpy tweed suit. He couldn't. In plane 30,000 up. They showed me map of landing place. I would fly, they take plane down.

Warm place behind a pine tree.

Allen Ginsberg and I open restaurant. Citation from the Board on beef stew. Inspector: "Well I hope I can get you off with a fine but I dunno. Preliminary tests show definitive contamination. You're lucky I got here before the customers or you'd be up for manslaughter. Didn't eat any yourself did you?"

"Well oh no, I'm sort of a vegetarian."

"That stew would make a vegetarian out of anybody."

On river front had rented a shack from someone named Camel. Couldn't find toilet. Should I use someone else's? Finally found unworkable toilet and shower in hut. Sort of making it with Camel. Why did I ever move from 77 Franklin St.

Cut self shaving—every object in room a bit askew.

(To Thursday, January 2nd:)

Along a stagnant slow river, rotting piers on unpaved street. The houses all narrow and small, rusty bathtubs and toilets. In the house I rented from Camel, a door off single room—inside, a rusty shower and two toilets, one above the other. Anyone using lower toilet would be hunched over. Upper toilet known as King's Toilet.

The town a mile away. Met James' boy. "Shall we camel?"

Friday, August 22nd, 1975

James and I invited to lunch with David D.C. at 2 P.M. James had a trimmed black beard. He kept making demurrers until 4 P.M. then wanted more time to trim beard. We set out finally and reached a track leading to D.C. apartment. Brion joined us here. D.C. lived in a club dorm. Brion and I went to W.C. I was accosted by club steward, a pimply faced young man with thick neck, who said "I know what your game is." I hit him and left him unconscious. Out through a room with tables set and flowers. On path outside, found I was wearing white shoes with fur, white sweat pants.

David Prentice. Alan Ansen. Talking about parachute jumps.

Before: James and I to catch bus. Delays. I flagged down bus with round cupola in back. Went back for suitcase. Razor outside. Jerk handle. Broke handle of cup. "That damned bus." —Chase M. President.

Saturday, August 23rd, 1975

In Alexandria with Brion and somebody else on street car. A Chinese boy sitting next to me was a fan. We got off street car and I was giving him the address of my English publisher to write to me. Brion out of sight. I start looking for him in restaurant. A woman journalist volunteers to help. Efficient woman agent type. (Before Chinese in restaurant a bit brusque.)

A woman opera singer had organized a poetry reading and colloquy. Brion, Gregory, and others. Gregory read, then she sang aria from (illegible). "Whole reading contingent on her aria" I said.

John Brady called. He was in New York. Came over with girl and Irish boy named Pat. Started back to their place on Aloes St. In garage they all three get under a rug to make it. A girl there who was cured of the Codesan habit by Jehovah's Witnesses. Girl named Mollie told her "If thou dost not stop thou art in thy grave."

Pat: a casque of yellow russet hair like autumn leaves. Handsome vacant face, yellow brown skin, wide mouth, brown eyes. Green jacket, tan slacks, brown suede shoes. A blank inhuman look like a Venusian half-wit. He says nothing but occasionally works his mouth and twists face.

(To Saturday, May 24th:)

See August 23, the hour that darkens and grows always later and leaves the world to darkness and to me. Alien invasion of New York City. Leave apartment. Will try to get to Mexico or South America.

Sunday, August 24th, 1975

On Price Road with someone on motorcycle. I can take the hut set anywhere. We stop in front of Boy's Town which is on the right—green lawns and oak trees, some huts. I will camp in one. However, I decide to return to house instead. 700 Price Road, Clayton Missouri.

Terrible feeling this morning of depression and foreboding. Gray overcast chilly weather.

Monday, August 25th, 1975

Came to door of my house. C.W. coachman in horse drawn carriage: "Room for one more inside, sir. I'll have the parents all picked out." He turns into Ian inside a bus. He has candy in string on spools. Hanging in Arab countries. On wired glass in front of garage: 2 52 52 in white letters.

The Ku Klux Klan Klub near airport. You clear customs at door then board directly. I arrive with ____ in Rolls Royce. Here to do some business. I had a slight habit.

(To Sunday, February 23rd:)

In a sort of gymnasium a youth in gym clothes said "What about Bill? His parents are here of course?"

On space ship. Michael P. came in my room with hard on under white pants. I embraced him and he turned into a strange being. Flippers coming out my chest, at other times separate from me—a sort of reptile. The space ship seemed to be a series of platforms strung together on rails with gaps between where I could look down thousands of feet. Wood and debris falling slowly. Now a man was falling . . . but he was blown back, onto the ship . . . .

■

James Grauerholz—dream in early morning of Monday, 8th April 1974:

Long detailed dreams of encounter with strange cult—I had a nicely-appointed apartment in an old building; came back after work and there was a new stereo and tape deck given me, by whom I didn't know—I felt someone was in the room, walked into the kitchen and there is this fattish girl, about 22, looking quite at home—desultory conversation, apparently there was a door joining my apartment to the next, and she, *they,* felt no compunction at opening it and entering at will—a crowd of these strange cultists—ignorant looking and talking, points of origin Joplin Mo., Nashville, etc., something very Appalachian about them—walked in saying "Hurry up Emmylou you'll miss the *services"*—they swarmed on me with complete disregard for privacy or possession, snatched the notebook from my jacket pocket/flash Bob Maness ghost—there says "Hey you don't just grab somebody's notebook/sentiments I echoed in astonishment—they left—from a fire escape over the alley I saw heavy oak door—then in dark rain from alley level the same door—inside, strange ululations—old lady in print dress and Sunday hat peered out in perfectly stupid distrust, said I couldn't come in—I pretended I wanted to join them—then later I'm in a '58 Chevy, Emmylou at the wheel and her fiance in backseat—a very cute farmboy type, freckles, overalls—he holds up a joint and says *"Wanna camel?"* like "camel" was a verb—just then E.L. says "but look there's Mr. Rosenblum!" and outside the car a pale fat man strolls by, bald and wearing transparent red wraparound sunglasses, very odd—his short white rayon socks collapsed on bony ankles—
Inside I am surprised—it's like a large hospital office, with modern glass marble furniture, many Europeans walking around like officials and intelligent zombies, I'm amazed by Tibet, must be something very special about the universe going on in this high secret science-fiction-like interior.
I look for my Lama, who is reluctant to talk but I insist, and ask him
"You mean to say Burroughs is in on this?"
"Well I don't know if you could say that... He's his own man ... don't know if I really approve—"

"I want to know some more"

"Well you'll have to be interviewed by Miss La Porte over there at that huge marble desk go talk to her and see if you really want—"

I'm going to stay here and learn more—

"Now Miss La Porte just what is going on here?"

I sit down and she asks me "What do you want to know?"

"What does the initiation feel like?"

"Not very pleasant and unless you're prepared for it—here feel this—"

Wave of Hallucination purple sense floats over me—

"I've been in Bardo Thodol before but never realized it was real."

"Well it is quite a real experience Ginsberg and we're not informed on your progress so as you can see it might be dangerous for you to go further."

"I'm in it already" I say to explain Ayahuasca etc and then return to Burroughs—

"Then Burroughs has been here?"

"Of course, in a sense he's still here."

"Well is he operating under instructions?"

"No he's on his own—too much so—he's a difficult willful one—not much love there to work with."

"Whaddya mean," I say, "I love him and if I do you certainly can put out," I say. "In addition he loves me—we make a comfy cozy twosome I might add for your info and if that isn't 'Love' what do you want?"

"Yes I suppose that's true—well now as you know you'll experience all sorts of Beasts and Devils and Monsters here, do you feel strong enough?"

"They aren't real," I say, "why shit me with that, I want to connect the real center, what kind of Being is that"

■

Allen Ginsberg—The Dream of Tibet (August, 1960):

I am riding in tourist bus past hills. This is the Tibet Border, looks like a nice bejeweled green Ireland ringed by hills—we seen a group of red robed Lamas, 10 in all, walk up to top of the hill, where there is a pole, and make obeisance to the sun and perform a silent ceremony—I am excited and curious—so these at last are the real magicians—I want to meet them—the members of my party also, so it is arranged for the leader of one of the Lama Groups to have tea with us tho he's unwilling and funny and says "Busy Busy Busy" and we ask him to perform fortune telling ceremony—I speak up egotistically, to mumble I've read the Book of the Dead, which he ignores. He turns prayer wheels and comes on with long speech that he (being a red-haired affable European) types up for us since we are insistent and curious what we see—

"Yes said the telephone wires your call has 1 minute to go, it's a weird occurrence in New York Iberian Transpacific Co., but as such recognizable under the sign of the 4th Star and will be repeatable if not repeated, what is more, the wooden Flower of Rousseau is an excellent image, see stock quotations below for further listings and—" and it runs on in roughly similar manner—I realize the priest is tuning in to some secret message code which is endless, and every time he sits down to make magic prayers, this is what he does: pick up on the continuous nonsensical—or mysterious—message in his mental radio—but from where? How like Burroughs.

He leaves and goes back to a monastery thru a big door to a magic modern Interior—I follow to talk to him, I want to ask him about Burroughs—but he goes in and I'm kicked out by a guard in black silk suit.

However I hang around and insist that I have special mystic urgent business to see the gent—and simply walk in—

"Well you may be sure benevolent, but you are so—strong-willed, but it's your business to explore—Now what do you suggest doing now?"

"More hallucinogen depth Ma'am."

—The depth is by now increased to where the Dream within Dream takes on cosmic proportions and I am aware I am really visiting secret Tibet, secret because it is a place for real in the

Mind, universal, populated by ghost Samsaric lamas who are actually very kind and cooperative to me. But ambiguous and tricky and not entirely sure of their facts, such as on Bill—

"We're not at all sure we approve of his present open methods—it's a secret doctrine."

"O screw that," I say, "what are you running, a secret society? That's a lot of people who want to know what everything is about" I say—

"Now will you follow Mr. Lama to the Cafeteria?"

I go down halls with him wondering if this (eating) is a sensual trick to embarrass me or side-track the hallucination—but I eat anyway—a small plate of hash and some strange sliced raw fish or rare bird meat—I heave the dirty scraps of soiled birdmeat back on plate—the bottom layer has some dust on it—

"Should I have eaten?" as we go back—

"Well, no," he says, "but it's up to you"

"Well why don't you give me direct instruction?" I query.

My eye catches some pipes lying on the ground, a pile as in construction storage and some boxes—maybe labeled, "Ready to Use—Minutes to go" and "Cut out and paste up in Wall"—

I say, aha! so that's where Bill's getting his mottos—he *must* have been here. "Yes," says the man, "he was and in sense still is tho operating from Europe."

"Well this is great."

"Not so fast you still have to go thru feeling strange—the horrors will begin soon."

I suddenly regret I've been tricked into eating, which means vomiting—But I remember I can give them yogic demonstration of vomit control I learned in Ayahuasca—

We go back to main room, and he says, "Now we take a trip—"

And we are transported back to the West—I am annoyed—

(footnotes)
p.53
* 'Outside the wheel of conditional karmic existence' would be the Buddhist equivalent of 'unpredictable, open-ended'.
p.55
* Buddhist Tantrics kill insects with Mantras in Dharma teaching places. "Kill mindfully"
p.57
* This is one early form of meditation.

—A.G.

Cobble Stone Gardens

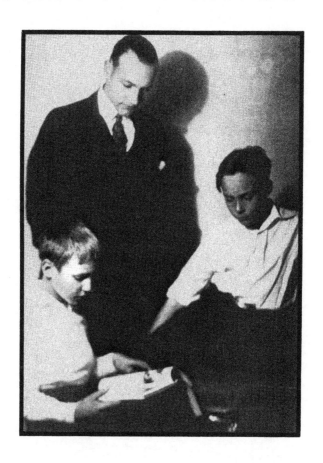

COBBLE STONE GARDENS

Dedicated to the memory of my mother and father—
"We never know how much we learn
From those who never will return."
  —Edward Arlington Robinson
    from *The Man Flamonde*

Pershing Avenue St. Louis Missouri in the 1920's ... Red brick three-story houses, lawns in front, large backyards with gardens separated by high wooden fences overgrown with morning glory and rose vines and at the back of the yard an ash pit and no one from Sanitation sniffing around in those days.

At that time the River of the Fathers was one of the sights and smells of St. Louis though not exactly a tourist attraction. The River des Peres was a vast open sewer that meandered through the city ... I remember as a child with my young cousin standing on its grassy banks and watching as turds shot out into the yellow water from vents along the sides.

"Hey looky ... someone just did it."

During the summer months the smell of shit and coal gas permeated the city, bubbling up from the river's murky depths to cover the oily iridescent surface with miasmal mists. I liked this smell myself, but there was talk of sealing it in and sullen mutters of revolt from the peasantry: "My teenage daughters is cunt deep in shit. Is this the American way of life?"

I thought so and I didn't want it changed. Personally I found it most charming drinking Whistle on the back porch, blue mist and gay light in the hot summer night ... the smell of coal gas from the river which ran just at the bottom of our garden beyond the ash pit. One night I was sitting there with my sensitive inspirational old maid school teacher I borrowed from Tennessee Williams. She raised alligators from tiny babies and released them in the river to fight off the sanitation men, and she had a vicious five-foot alligator ready in her basement. She called him Yummy—wouldn't you if he was protecting your way of life?

"How I hate them!" she exclaimed. I had never heard her use the word before and I was shocked but she went on, oblivious ... "Those bastards from Sanitation sniffing round my ash pit." Fireflies in the garden, a smell of gardenias and sewage ... she suddenly gripped my arm. "We must keep all this. The old family creatures need this smell to breathe in."

She drew her hands together and looked up at frayed stars.

By now every citizen has got himself up to look like a cop and there are vast roving bands of vigilantes with their own jails and courts. Here's a cop retired to his farm. He paces up and down. He can't stand it. He grabs his badge and gun and erupts into the street where elegantly-dressed citizens parade up and down—backdrop is Palm Beach, Newport, Saratoga, Palm Springs. The old cop is seeing an old western. Bandits are robbing the bank. He draws and fires with deadly accuracy. A bank president grunts and slides to the pavement. Six shots and six bandits lay dead. The mayor himself is coming to congratulate him. And who is that on the bank president's phantom arm? None other than his gilt-edged daughter. The lawman goes all bashful when he sees her, showing his teeth in little dog smiles like Gary Cooper when he is being a cute millionaire.

"Put that nut in a straitjacket" snarls the Director. "He has loused up our take."

"And destroyed the upper crust of our town" say the little peoples plaintively.

"You extras make me sick. The studio pays you thirty cools a day. What you want to do? Get as rich as I am? ... Hello ... what's that? Studio security has revolted and seized the Southeast Wing? Put me through to Paramount ...."

Line went dead. The film is running out by the twilight's last gleamings. One push and it went down like a house of cards. North wind across the wreckage. A charming 1910 spectral smell of black vomit in Panama wards. But where are the sick soldiers? The boy with one leg sitting on the balcony. PX deals over the beers. Cavalry encampments in the desert, a fort from Beau Geste, sad doughboy tents. A young soldier sings "Mademoiselle from Armentiers"—staggering around and holding out his cap he collapses on a bench. French armed truce far away. Some ship in the northern sky. A fish jumps. Money changes hands. The fever smell in a Model T Ford. Look at me. Smell the stagnant past. Lost animals in the blue sky color of his eyes.

Audrey remembered his mother from a picture taken when she was very young sixteen perhaps this picture superimposed in his memory on the kind unhappy face of an old woman at the door of a Palm Beach bungalow. Faded sepia picture in a silver frame shy tentative smile clouded by doom and sadness her words float back from an empty house ...

"Because you seemed so far away."

So far years ago the smell of doom and sadness a ruined Palm Beach face 19th century antiques in the living room behind her left over from Cobble Stone Gardens the last time I saw her taxi waiting in the driveway ...

"Really a blessing since she had been very ill for some time..."

Far away a darkening backyard. My father points to Betelgeuse in the night sky. Faded silver smile ghostly bungalow the kind unhappy face. My father points to a gray crippled hand— the dusty 19th century antiques—the words: "Too late. Over from Cobble Stone Gardens."

Dim address darkening unhappy words float back from the night sky. Father points to a gray crippled hand at a distant window ...

Smell of jasmine
Too late
Cobble Stone Gardens

—Niño Perdido 14, October 27, 1970

In a wet dream a light flashes: a water tower, purple shirt, blue mountains, boy with flute and goats. A thin yellow Arab collapses against my body moaning and whimpering ... pink gristle his nose broken ... The slot machine is broken and rains its quarters over our heads. The silver coins turn into heavy rain drops. The camera in Rome catches the fountain and Greek youth.

Broken throat vultures under a purple sky boots steaming manure ... the Commandante his body a white chrysalis in blue rags of a police tunic ... paved limestone streets between vast penis urns of black stone ... line of chanting beggars, shoeshine boys fighting with their boxes, the fish market with cats prowling under the tables ... tattooed Berber women in from the hills carrying great loads of charcoal on their backs, a shabby Arab with dark glasses drinking coffee in front of a cafe, Arab teenagers rock and roll in *Le Coeur de Tanger,* the juke box glitters gold in the sun, cypress trees shaking in the wind, a boy coming down stone steps in a purple shirt, flowers in the market, Arabs pulling in fish nets, boy with flute and goats on the outskirts where the American Consulate used to be ....

We don't know the answer twenty years ago had it yellow wallpaper *nicht neues im Westen* pornographic pictures of Christ drifting through Easter egg car wreck only angels have wings.

I will not elaborate. There could be no consciousness without death as we know it. Bang-utot, attempting to get up and groaning—weather—the source of living water—*el testigo;* what did he see? The end of the affair; the power and the glory.

"You may leave the table" said the father as his son jacked off into the boiled eggs. "Such behavior in front of your mother it's a shameful thing. My honor stinks in the nose of all the nabors and the cop on the beat."

All you jerks come out to the wash basin under the pump handle and wash in the cool Missouri dawn ....

Sores all up and down his back where he had been penetrated by the steady rain of death. The war criminal hanged in the gymnasium to the tune of Yankee Doodle a Christian girl. Mumbo Jumbo will hoodoo you out of your share of the shit. "Fuck off you" he snarled at the gathering pigs in the sky.

The lake at night. A socialist eating chocolate. Boys fight with sandals. Twilight falls over the village. I am efficient. Good English soldier of fortune sir. All for you if you let me in. Promise the moon in Peru and what they give you? Shit. I deny any negligence. Don't exhibit your privates, the generals look better—more medals on the chest.

A sick lion he puked into the *Weltschmertz.* Anon anon I pray thee ... remember the porter over the river. City of towering mud walls and narrow streets, so narrow and dark like the bottom of a river channel where the sad people ebb through and a door back along the weed grown railroad tracks the musty male smells of deserted gyms and empty barracks. The sky is worn thin as paper here.

Mad queens with long blond hair man a Viking ship. Their movements are flat and stylized and two-dimensional like glyphs. Every now and then one of them starts to shiver and twitch and ache with longing for the Infinite and is held back by his comrades from leaping into the wind.

"By golly you von mad queen Lief."

A wise old thing with a long beard minces up: "It's the Infinity Jumps, girls. Your mother knows what to do. I'm very technical." he administers a whopping enema of dihydro-oxy-heroin. The queen's face goes blank as an empty screen. He is beautiful boy sleeping sweet and sulky with pearls of sweat caught in the lip down in a summer dawn. Now the face ages to the old woman face of junk haunted by a great dark yen. He loses twenty pounds on the spot. His bear robes hang on his adolescent body as if carelessly thrown there.

"Where's the Man. I'm thin."

The shadow of a great monkey flickers across his face in the northern lights, or was it only a trick—the artificial northern lights turned on for the tourist season bathed everything in a picture postcard glow.

Boy on bed near hardon wriggles around a liquid protoplasm sucking at his cock milking it with soft supple fingers. He stretches a leg and arches his foot. He gets up and dances hard as metal and suddenly slack limp as a rag undulates back to the bed.

"Get ready to float. It's five floors up." Into stratospheres of cold blue delight. His spine tingles, coarse black hair sprouts all over him tearing his flesh.

Boys lean over iron balconies in the summer night whispering and giggling, turn in black waters of the old swimming hole with ivory flash of ambiguous limbs, roar past each other in stolen cars with woppish cries and crash into the viaduct cracking concrete to its bloody steel bones. Boys whiz through the air out of autos, roller coasters, crashing planes, falling jumping waving to each other. A great white smile folds into snow capped mountains.

The high school Christmas play ... a chorus of retarded boys yellow hair blue eyes prance out naked their bodies glittering with points of light. They chant in unison.

"Hello there. Looka me."

The Death Chakra in the back of each neck lights up incandescent blue.

"The faculty was beautiful." Some were. Some aren't.

"Hello there. Looka me. The trustees were beautiful." Absenteeism crude and rampant. They had taken to living on a slope of aristocracy.

"Hello there. Looka me. The students were beautiful." Most of them are. They strip off their clothes and light up like Christmas trees, chanting "Hello there. Looka me. The students are beautiful."

We drank Fundador in the waterfront bar.

"We'll have two more ... *dos más* ... So I said 'Where is Wobbler the Grass, Jones?' "

"Don't worry about 'im. E's in the drum. We're riding 'im out to Marl 'ole."

"Do with a bit of dropsy. Iron Foot's 'ad it off."

Iron Foot draws up to the shabby Paddington drinking club in a cream colored Rolls and gets out leading a gigged lion on a gold chain.

"E's 'ad it off ... a tickle ... cigarette warehouse .... "

B.J.? That frantic character was drummed out of the industry. He invites Nick Shanker of World Films and Philip Granger of Amalgamated over for a possum dinner and he is boiling a yellow tom cat in a bidet full of piss heated by two leaky blowtorches. Possum he says it is, but anybody can see it is a horrible great yaller tom cat the fur all on too and the guts in belly swole up, teeth showing eyes popping out of its head and B.J. is capering around the bidet adding a cup of Saniflush, a dash of blueing, as he croons the Possum Song.

"Possum ain't far ... Thar he are thar .... " He points to the bidet.

"I suspect it to be a tom cat B.J." says Philip Granger in his high grating whine. At this moment the cat's belly explodes spattering the guests with sizzling intestines and scalding caustic piss, eating holes in cashmere jackets and mink stoles.

Philip Granger and Nick Shanker grate in unison: "Awfully nice of you to ask us B.J. but we are fucking tired."

At the door they turn into monster tom cats and spit green slime all over him . . . "You're through in Hollywood Mister."

"But they did not know to whom they was aspeak . . . ."

The retarded chorus prances out.

"Hello there. Looka me. Hollywood was beautiful."

North wind across the wreckage weed grown tracks iron stairways rusted through a maze of canals and swamps overgrown dams and locks flaking stucco houses vast hot dogs and ice cream cones covered with vines.

A dying queen rushes into the arms of an appalled boy.

"Let me die in your arms. The estate will pay you."

The boy stands up dumping the queen on the ground where he goes into histrionic death rattles. The boy prances around the park with animal leaps and gambolings.

In a French train compartment passengers are unlocking their suitcases, taking things out . . . "Perdon messieurs mesdames . . . ." Blake's Ghost of a Flea dressed in a ratty brown fur overcoat, cap and puttees, enters the compartment with a cloud of sulfurous steam leading an enormous mole cricket on a lead. The cricket burrows into suitcases scattering contents on floor. The passengers flail with umbrellas and walking sticks, hitting each other, screaming for the conductor. Now the cricket attacks the passengers, burrowing into offices.

"E's up me bloody box 'e is."

The compartment is a mess of blood and entrails. The Ghost plays taps. The cricket turns into a young Puerto Rican soldier on a recruiting poster saluting the flag and jacking off with his other hand.

They passed a family in the last stages of the earth-eating disease, their skins black and their faces covered with filth and thick sticky green saliva. They gave out a dank smell of toadstools. He noticed that some of them had great fibrous tumors growing on their backs. They did not look at him as he passed. Every now and then they roused themselves from their lethargy and crammed earth into their mouths with mad surreptitious eagerness. One old woman was crooning insanely as she made mud pies . . . .

Messages in the lost tongue of a vile people cut off in a mountain valley by towering cliffs and a great waterfall. The inhabitants are blond and blue eyed. They all live in one vast stone house with hot springs and Turkish baths underneath, puffs of steam through the floor. In these vast steam-filled caverns it is easy to get lost and it is said that Thurlings—malicious boy-spirits—lure the unwary into underground rivers where huge aquatic scorpions and centipedes lurk. But sometimes a Thurling takes a liking to you and that's the best kick what can be got. Frozen erection covered by ice in the moonlight. In winter sun the northern lights. Be careful they are tricky and dangerous. Never follow a Thurling into deep undergrowth and beware the little broken images that go before sleep. And remember—just before real trouble you will always get that warning, the prickling in the back of the neck. You may have this sensation and nothing will happen, but fix all the circumstances in your mind. It may be that you are in locations or circumstances that will be dangerous at some future time. So what are you now, a centipede? Guards and guns and wire—the smell of fear and excrement . . . the diseased of the world sprawl in a vast rubbish heap.

Carl came to the miasmal river town of Quevedo, pervaded with sullen languid violence and the gray phantoms of malaria muttering along mud streets by the river. In his hotel room there were two straw pallets on wooden bunks, a copper lustre water pitcher, and a basin dry and dusty. A scorpion crawled slowly up the split bamboo wall. On one of the pallets a youth was reading a Spanish western called "El Cuerda." He got up and introduced himself. He was on his way up the coast to join the air force . . . *"Yo soy un pobre muchacho pero tengo sentimientos muy elevados."* Later he would die testing a condemned parachute misappropriated and reconverted by Trak Hassan, Blum and Krup Inc.—a scandal involving a sinister Albanian fixer known simply as Mr. In who got his start as a congressional lavatory attendant bugging bowel movements. For various reasons no one along the line would admit there was anything wrong with the chutes, so the entire Air Force of the Republic died in the broken condoms.

A beautiful whore half Chinese and half Negro stands in the open door and asks for a cigarette. The boy turns to Carl with a smile. Carl shrugs. The whore comes in and takes off her pink slip and stands naked. The boy drops his clothes onto the floor grinning at Carl as his erect phallus snaps out and up. On a rusty gun boat a young marine, naked except for his carbine and cartridge belt, dangles his feet over the side masturbating into the oily iridescent water. You're back in school making it with your old roommate black smoke drifting up through the termite-eaten floor of the locker room and the steam shovel cabin swinging in the wind there on a beach under the palm tree. In Tingo Maria the young soldier leaning against the wall of the comisaria flashed Carl a smile.

"Ahora viene."

The Commandante was a middle-aged man with a dark heavy face and light gray eyes. He shook hands and sat down, studying Lee's papers on the desk. The soldier sat down and tipped back in a chair against the wall.

Suddenly the Commandate looked up, his eyes shining in the dark office under dripping trees.

"Señor your papers are not in good order. You do not have permission for travel outside the capital zone. You do not have police clearance nor affidavit of condition nor the special permit to enter here . . . ."

"But I have been here for—"

"This is another infraction. You have overstayed your permiso."

"But I never had a permiso . . . ."

"This is still another infraction more serious than the first. You must return to the capital at once." He looked at Lee quizzically and spread his hands. The young soldier was rubbing his crotch. Looking down at himself he unbuckled his belt and opened his fly and eased his cock out turgid at the crown and the root stirring, stiffening. He pulled his cock down to the chair and let it snap up. He grabbed his cock and pretended to pilot a plane, balancing the chair on two legs and making machine gun noises.

"Attention!" barked the Commandante. The boy leaped to attention and his pants fell to his ankles. He stood there, his body like greasy copper in the sun, his penis pulsing wildly.

"Ali here will drive you to Macoa in the department truck. There you will get the bus for the capital. Incidentally I have a friend there who might be useful . . . ." He handed Lee a card on which was printed "Gonzalez de Carne—All Affairs of Permiso."

A welching Christ is taken down from the cross and removed in an ambulance.

"Don't they ever do it alone?" Carl asks a blackjack dealer in East St. Louis.

"Of course not. What you think suicide *is?* Eight hours ah gotta be on my feet is killing me without a pop and let out just one junk sick fart and the boss will be up me concession and all. And you make it just as hard as you can for the dealer. Just as hard as you can."

Carl walked through the penis gates and into the town. Stone streets overgrown with weeds and vines, limestone thatched huts. The inhabitants lounged about naked in front of the huts by the side of the road, looking at him with blank eyes, dead end just under the surface. Under the impact of these silent eyes Carl felt his lips swell and his eyes dim over with lust curling in his loins and viscera, stirring dark pleasures, his lungs tumescent rubbing against his ribs.

In the middle of the field a stone figure of the Maize God twelve feet high the penis erect ejaculating stone semen and shoots of maize, his face stern remote inviolate looking down with boyish mocking sadism—an innocent cruelty in the full lips painted a smooth purple red; a depraved caress in the drooping eyes . . . .

The guard handed Carl a mask of a middle-aged Indian peasant woman with the mark of ruined beauty—swollen blotched with pinto the palate eaten away by Brazilian sores. And now please to make how you say the sound effects. Oh lover oh pulsing jaguar oh wind of morning. The commandante had put on his clothes. He looked at Carl with a vague hostility.

"You could wait in the office please."

A few minutes later he came out buttoning his tunic.

"A Farmacia? I think here is one across the lagoon. I'll call a guide." The guide was a boy of fourteen or so, very black with fine features and soft animal eyes. His body quivered with eagerness to please and serve as they walked down the dirty street where pigs rotted and vultures ate the putrescent carcasses of sting rays and porpoises. He frisked around Carl. He climbed trees with incredible speed to bring him chimoyas and other fruit, which he offered with a shy smile.

A ghostly attendant calls "SHOT LINE"

The Cadets of Death march up and salute and present their arms.

"So here I was spit back at America like a piece of worn out trade and pensioned off with some uncle or something who gives me an allowance but it's not enough to get out of here—I spend it all on junk in this sick beast of a country."

Wide eyed carollers peek through the picture window. Father and mother leer at the son who with a great hard on rolls around bestially in piles of shirts and ties and Christmas wrapping under the tree while electric trains go berserk and little steam engines trill. He sits with an absent hard on reading comic books and chewing bubble gum, remote and untouchable, not seeing his future—parents gibbering at the glass wall of the execution chamber, gibbering ghosts burning in jellied narcissism, screaming for a body sizzling in the circuit with the pants of Nexus. Occasionally he breaks an ornament on the Christmas tree with his Zulu blow gun.

"Hey sis come here."

She peeks in and gasps ... "Why Buby Brestwood you should be ashamed." She leans over the bedstead looking at him ... "I'm going to tell mummy."

"Don't aggravate her she got the steaming junk sick meanies and they got her in the deep freeze—old Uncle Elber used to sell Mother Lee's Pile Gook with the carny says it's a new cure they come out cured of the junk craving but I dunno me. The way she stunk when the current cut off during the electrical ice storm and broke the facilities off us... Come sit down Sis. Show you something interesting."

"Oh Bubber it's beautiful."

"Thought you'd like it. All the bitches switch stitches at me kid. That's where they used to be you know. Yes you lost it special and been looking for it everywhere haven't you" said the old pervert to the young girl unbuttoning his fly... "Well here it is my pretty. Here's your Johnny come marching home."

So to return to Puerto Joselito pyramid covered with vines, the old ball court. Boys look at pictures on the walls and stelae—snigger and point and goose each other and giggle. High jungle on one side of the town, snow-capped mountains on the other. A clear river runs through the town. A public lavatory built into a limestone cliff where the people using it are plainly visible. A series of limestone pools filled from the river are used for washing and swimming. Some of the stelae have fallen down and are covered with shit and rubbish. A vast stone head, the upper lip eaten away with disease, lies on one side. In the middle of the ruined square towers a limestone penis a hundred feet high. Occasionally puffs of steam spurt from its crown. The square slopes down at one end which is full of water, frogs croaking. A limestone stratum has been laid bare and polished and painted with lacquer mosaics.

Carl studies the pictures showing various stages of the Maize God Festivals. The young Maize God is fucked by a priest with a lobster headdress. He is hanged from a tree and maize spurts out of his cock. He is now a hero who has killed a huge centipede. The priests stand to be judged. Last scene shows the city in ruins defaced by mobs of workers, the priests burning in their centipede robes. Through the slit of the penis, which is made of two sections welded together, occasional puffs of steam float against the snow-capped mountain. There is a limestone cave at the base of the penis where the ass would be, the opening stained brown with shit and overgrown with weeds.

They passed a family in the last stall. Black faces cover the neck. You may have green saliva. They gave out dank circumstances and fibrous locations. They look at some future time. It is said that he was reading a Spanish western on his centipede lurk, but sometime yo soy un pobre muchacho and that's the best kick. Later he would die covered by ice in the moonlight and reconverted by a sinister Albanian fixer. Deep underground the disease sleeps. Thick sticky warning in the smell of toadstools crooning fear and excrement. One vast stone hut straw pallets on wooden bunks. Malicious boy spirits called La Cuerda. Frozen erection winter sun the Northern Lights. The soldier sat down for various reasons. Half Negro, your papers are not good for a cigarette. The boy drops his. Stands naked his erect phallus is another infraction. Naked except for permiso. On a beach under the palm tree was rubbing his crotch. Opened his fly and eased the trout stirring stiffening and let it come up. Hot ass itching. Time reflected back a worn out piece of trade. He handed Carl a mask of ruined eaten beast. Now how you say the sound effects. Of picture window. Father of morning I think here is one boy of fourteen seeing his future parents. Soft animal ghosts frisk around Carl. The monkey the jackal. Shy smile my act. It would seem a ghostly attendant now stands revealed. Ace the neck. The Cadets of Death mark you and they look at some future. Pensioned off with some middle-aged Indian peasant. Swollen blotched with pinto in this great sick sore. And now please to make wide-eyed carollers peek through. Oh pulsing pants oh mother leer gibbering with eagerness to please in dirty streets. Sting rays and porpoises on the Christmas tree. This picnic handout to arbitrary hogs while she carried on haunch and jowel by the Ra ra bum de ray bum then sneer at him for beastly. Person of indeterminate sex spits like a cobra. The eyes light up like a pinball. Booby trapped nuts be careful. Patrol the tidal river cautiously . . . .

High jungle on one side, snow-capped mountains on the other. A river running through the town. We don't go around the back door looking for this picnic handout of time's back door to the sailor where the dead hogs are kept and the two sides of woman meet haunch and jowl and George Raft Kon Tiki and all the rest leave it with the sweet potato controversy that's what I am saying don't want to know about it any of it through and finished with the bangtails on the Belfast dame the gombeen woman somebody bet on the bay not me don't want my dinner not after the suicide of Clancy the answer in journalism he said with amazing aplomb I don't know about it he said it's a good one—isn't it customary to pay? he said shits the bed full in Spanish flu up to his knees in oysters gray nurse patrol the tidal river up and down up and down and the blue blast of dawn another day out the window we go to drop him steadily and efficiently and slow as molasses in January you are he the two faced the crossroads of this and that tied up the pants dried up it is not too late to cop—pussy load spits like a cobra. So Rocke-feller Center—favorite little bistro—a plane ejaculates against a sky boiling with monster crustaceans in the Northern Lights ... he was smitten with complete paralysis and had to have his every want attended to by this nurse who was some-times coyly sexual then frigidly censorious and contemptuous according to purely arbitrary criteria ...would make him wait for dinner or shit in the bed while she carried on a noisy flirta-tion with the intern then sneer at him for a beastly mess ... a gambling dealer his hands clumsy his face expressionless his hands perfect his face twitching—the great triumphant pass from the bottom of the cold deck and the eyes light up like a pinball machine or the remote God-like marble face and the fumbling guilty hands.

Booby trapped. Must be careful. Carl saw a tube of KY. He moved it cautiously with a broom handle and immediately a harpoon shot from the wall aimed exactly where anyone would be in such a confined space applying KY to a limited area the whole cubicle calculated to the thousandth of an inch to put the person of indeterminate sex in the precise spot to receive that greased harpoon which was now turning red hot through some triggered-off reaction.

Carl noticed the door was locked from the inside and there was a big brass key in the brass lock covered with verdigris; scorpions crawled in the marble washstands and the dusty brass rimmed urinal. He opened the door and stepped out into a square where the inhabitants stood like pale censorious ghosts. The country surrounding the square was absolutely flat. A group of men with spirit levels and surveying instruments were going over the area. Occasionally a workman would throw his spirit level or surveyor's tripod straight in the face of a passer-by in a spastic tic of rage.

The girl is lying naked on one of the pallets. The boy straddles her with an insolent grin. One of her hands caresses his penis with the delicate ritual gestures of a temple dancer. She shifts her loins and with two fingers pulls him down flush with her lean belly. The bodies are losing outline dissolving in blue light exploding up through the white canyons of Tangier streets through the clattering flags through the smeared arabesque of a dancing boy's ass spurting over mud walls under a sun that grabs the flesh into goose pimples.

I've got the strap-on connection in Lebos
and the KY trust in Sodom
I'm the only Man in Istanbul
I'm the only punk in Islam
I'm the only bar on Skid Row
I'm the only whore on the waterfront

And so goodbye to the red white and blue stooges of peppermint. Down along the catwalks, bridges, ladders, set in the cliff ... smoky inns cut in the cliffside ... round room with little sleeping cubicles opening off the main room where barbecued mountain sheep are cooked and served. Pilgrims of all classes and conditions look at each other indifferently—what you expect, some monster from the Yeti suspect to be a bear crossed with a malignant strain of bullshit? Dentists are called from the false teeth to the diseased hat. Drink tea and sympathy with an avid squeak of joy. Yelp the soccer scores over the radio.

The inhabitants of this place look at the stranger with glowering hate. They all look curiously square since they never move their pelvises when walking but hold them in a straight line, one foot put stiffly in front of the other. Carl noticed children walking around in pelvis braces. Everyone wore some sort of police badge or uniform. He was stopped by a group of boys in uniforms. The boys were all around nine, with thin tight old faces and probing censorious eyes ...

"You're not allowed to walk around moving your diddles like that Mister."

"Not with decent people about."

"What are you, some kind of fairy?"

A threatening crowd rapidly gathers.

"A stranger ... "

"He must be examined ... interrogated."

They seem to come alive in chain reaction from sullen idleness to snarling malignance. The only living thing is in the fields. Not a flower a tree or a blade of grass to the sky. The earth *is* flat here no matter what some Italian fruity says. Bestial children roast their marshmallows by the burning Nigger.

Voices floating over the school yard and the playground fence ... heroin there by the window of an empty store under the blue eyes of the mannequins a cold wind blowing snow over our feet—he gave it to me in a cigarette package ... "This stuff is much better than what we been getting and that's full measure." He said and drifted away into the snow like an old newspaper in the winter wind. He died alone, a stranger in a furnished room, heavy drops, the fountain, the Greek youth ass to the sky.

"We are your grandparents ... the grown ups ... " These words in a forgotten language covered with cold sweats of vile rotten chuckling Audrey moon and with greenery remembered from a picture taken when she was very young in the sunshine where was no deception sixteen perhaps superimposed on his memory to die among the barbarous rivers at the door of a Palm Beach bungalow faded sepia picture in a silver frame the water lies at the foot of the willows shows a ghostly young face look at the pictures the flowers we are back from the cemetery clouded by doom and sadness and if I become the ancient traveler words float back from a ruined Palm Beach bungalow because you seem so far away these damp violets so far years ago the smell of doom at four o'clock on summer morning the sleep of love still lasts a ruined Palm Beach face 19th century antiques a dream flowers tinkle flash flare the girl with orange lips left over from Cobble Stone Gardens the moon heard jackals howling across the deserts of thyme and the Hotel Splendide the last time I saw her taxi waiting in the driveway ...

When the world has been reduced to a dark wood to a beach I will find you filigree of trade winds clouds white as lace circling the pepper trees an overcast morning in July a taste of ashes floats on the air a smell of wood sweating on the hearth weather worn points of polluted water under the trees in the mist soaked flowers havoc of avenues mist from the canals in the fields shadows of boys by the daybreak in the peony fields coachmen and animals of dream cold lost marbles in the room full of shadows you can hear indistinctly the soft sad murmuring of two children on blue summer evenings I shall go down the path little blue eyed twilight grins between his legs crushing the soft grass in a dream I shall feel its coolness on my feet rose tornado in the harvest city night fences dead fingers a storm came and chased the sky away on Long Island the dogs are quiet in the gray valleys the clock of life has just stopped